# FRANK

## GUARDIAN DEFENDERS

## KRIS MICHAELS

*This book is dedicated to Gary J.
Thank you for restoring my confidence. You will be missed, my friend. May you rest in peace.*

# THE CAST OF THE GUARDIAN WORLD

**Jacob King** (Code Name: **Alpha**, and is known as *Skipper* to Alpha Team)

He is married to **Victoria "Tori" (Marshall) King**. They have four sons, Talon, twins Trace and Tanner, and Tristan.

**Joseph King** (Code Name: **Fury**)

He is married to **Ember (Harris) King**. They have one son, Blake, and a daughter, Beth.

**Doctor Adam Cassidy** (Known as **Doc** to Alpha Team)

He is married to **Keelee (Marshall) Cassidy**. They have one daughter, Elizabeth (Lizzy).

**Jason King** (Code Name: **Archangel**)
He is married to **Faith (Collins) King**. They have three sons, Reece, Royce, Rogan and a daughter Rachel.

**Jared King** (Domestic Operations CEO. **Dom Ops**)
He is married to **Christian (Koehler) King** (No Code Name). They have one son, Marcus.

**Jasmine King** (Jazz)
She is married to **Chad Nelson**. They have a daughter, Chloe, and a son, Chance.

**Jewell Reynolds-King** (Code Name: **CCS**)
She is married to **Zane Reynolds** (Code Name: **Bengal**)

**Jade Demarco-King** (No Code Name, and she's not happy about this.)
She is married to **Nicolas (Nic) DeMarco**. (Together they are Domestic Operations Chief Operations Officers)

**Doctor Maliki Blue** (Mercy Team)
He is married to **Poet Campbell**, who is also **Mercy Team**.

**Frank Marshall** (Owner of the Rocking M Ranch)
He is married to **Amanda King**.

**Justin King** (Code Name: **Magus**)
He is married to **Danielle (Dani Grant) King**. They have one son, Wyatt.

**Drake (Simmons) Marshall**
He is married to **Doctor Jillian (Law) Marshall**.

**Dixon (Simmons) Marshall**
He is married to **Joy** (Code Name: **Moriah**) **Marshall**. They have a daughter, Kai.

**Mike White Cloud** (Code Name: **Chief**)
He is married to **Tatyana (Taty) Petrov**.

**Kaeden Lang** (Code Name: **Anubis**)
He is married to **Sky Meyers**. They have one daughter, Kadey.

**Isaac Cooper** (Code Name: **Asp**)
He is involved with **Lyric Gadson**.

**Ryan Wolf** (Code Name: **Lycos**)

He is married to **Bethanie Clark**. They have one son, **Ethan**.

**Dolan McDade** (Code Name: **Thanatos**)
He is married to **Eve Salutem**.

**Luke Wagner** (Code Name: **Tempest**), now a Sierra Team Member
He is married to **Pilar Grantham**.

**Dan Collins:** (Code Name: **Smoke**)
He is married to **Charley (Charlotte) Xavier** (Code Name: **Bambi**)

**John Smith** (Marshall Ranch Foreman)
He is married to **Shae Diamante** (Former Mossad).

**Doctor Jeremiah Wheeler** (Guardian Psychiatrist)
He is married to **Eden Wade**.

**The founder of Guardian and employer of many of the people mentioned above:**

**Gabriel Alexander** (David Xavier, Code Name: **The Saint**, previously known as **Archangel** before Jason took over as CEO of Guardian Security.) He is married to **Anna**. They have four children, **Gabrielle**, the oldest daughter, twin sons **Deacon and David (David goes by Ronan)**, and **Charlotte** (Charley).

# 1

*Present day, Marshall Ranch, South Dakota:*

Frank Marshall sat in front of the fire. The Christmas tree was lit, and the little ones were tucked into bed upstairs. He smiled and chuffed a laugh to himself. True, there were little ones, but most of his grandchildren were more adult than child.

He took a sip of the good stuff while Amanda poured herself a glass of wine. "It's good to have everyone home," she said as she sat beside him. He lifted his arm, and she slid next to him. A perfect fit, as always. He was thankful his daughter, Victoria, and her family had made the trip from the training complex in Arizona. She'd been through hell and hadn't felt strong enough to make the trip for Thanksgiving. The rest of the family who lived in Arizona—Joseph, Ember, and their kids—stayed with Tori, Jacob, and their children. That bastard Amari had messed with Tori's mind. His daughter had lived through things that no one should ever have to endure. She was strong, but damn it, his past and Tori's had reared their ugly heads and collided. The result had been catastrophic for his youngest. It nearly killed his girl. He'd never forgive himself for that.

"Tori looks good." Amanda sighed and took a sip of her drink.

"Thank you." They turned as Tori and her husband Jacob walked into the massive living room. "I'm better. I'm not ready to leave Arizona for more than a visit right now, but I'm making improvements." She laughed, adding, "With the help of pharmaceuticals."

Jacob's brow lowered. "That's nothing to poke fun at, babe. They help you. It doesn't matter what anyone thinks."

"I know. I guess I'm upset because I made it through the first event without meds."

"It doesn't make you weak. You're the strongest person I've ever known." He kissed her forehead, and she sighed and leaned into him.

"Join us for a while?" Amanda asked.

"Thank you. We need to let the horde fall asleep before bringing down the Santa gifts." Tori smiled, made her way to one of the nearby couches, and sat down.

Jacob attentively waited until she was on the couch before he went to the bar and poured himself a drink. Then he reached into the mini-fridge and grabbed sparkling water for Tori.

Gabriel and Anna strolled into the room next. His friend and his wife were more family than friends. Their kids, Ronan, Deacon, and Gabrielle, had joined them for the holiday at the ranch and were bunking with Jillian and Drake, who had no young ones who had aged out of the foster care system joining them until January. Gabriel's youngest, Charley, and her husband, Dan, had stayed in D.C. to keep the infrastructure build for Guardian moving through the holiday.

"Is this a party?" Gabriel asked.

Frank grunted, which made Tori laugh. God, he loved that sound.

"Was that a yes?" Anna chuckled.

"It was. Would you like some wine? I have a bottle or two of red in the fridge for you." Amanda leaned forward to set her glass down on the table.

"Stay seated, Amanda. I'll get it. Frank, where's the good stuff?" Gabriel headed for the bar as Anna sat on the far side of the couch that Frank and Amanda were sitting on.

"You ask like you don't know." Frank shook his head as he watched Gabriel go straight for the Pappy Van Winkle.

"Wait, he gets the good stuff?" Jacob's eyebrows flew up, an incredulous look plastered across his mug.

"Who does?" Jason and his wife Faith came into the room. Jason had been injured in that damn explosion during the Siege. He was walking with a cane now, a fancy gold-handled thing that had to have been made out of titanium to hold Jason's bulk.

"Gabriel," Jacob answered. He held up his drink. "Although, this scotch is smooth."

"If you say so." Jason lowered onto the couch where Tori and Jacob were sitting.

"Soda?" Faith asked after she put the baby monitor down on the table in front where Jason sat.

"Just water, please," Jason answered. His sobriety had been shattered when he was in the hospital after that building fell on him and the rest of the people from Guardian's Washington D.C. location. After back surgery many years ago, Jason had become addicted to Oxy, but he'd kicked it. The recent surgeries and pain pills had taken him back to step one, but he was determined to live sober. Jason didn't drink because he didn't want to risk substituting one addiction for another. The man had been through hell.

"How's Dani?" Faith asked as she sat by her husband with two water bottles.

"She's fine. Tired but fine. Her labor lasted just over twelve hours. Justin is in love with that little boy of theirs."

"What name did they settle on?" Anna asked as she took her glass of cold red wine from her husband.

"Wyatt Nathaniel King," Jacob said, lifting his glass. "To many more King and Marshall children."

Tori snorted, "Not from me."

"Or me," Faith agreed. "That angel in the bassinette upstairs is my last."

Jason reared back and stared at her. "We can't stop with a girl. We need another boy."

Faith turned to her husband. "Rachel is the last unless you push out the next one."

Jason smiled at his wife. "Birth control doesn't work for us. There will be another."

Faith made a snipping motion with her fingers. The horrified look that crossed Jason's face made everyone laugh.

"An invitation to the party would have been nice," Joseph said as he and Ember walked in with two boxes of presents.

"Has everyone else brought down Santa's gifts?" Ember asked as she knelt by the tree.

"Not yet. I don't trust my tribe. I'll wait an hour or so to make sure no one slips down that stairway."

Jacob laughed when Jason gave him a thumbs up and said, "Ditto."

"Where are Jared and Christian?" Tori looked around.

"They went over to Jasmine and Chad's. Christian wanted to see the new recording studio. Chad and Jasmine are leaving the day after Christmas to film a music special in Hollywood. It was the only time they could go over. They'll be back soon. Marcus has to be down for the count by now."

Amanda shifted, settling into Frank's chest more. He shifted to make her more comfortable. She added, "The rest of the crew will be here first thing in the morning. Now that Kai is finally sleeping through the night, Dixon and Joy weren't willing to mess up her schedule by spending the night here."

"I can't blame them. Reece didn't sleep through the night for almost a year." Faith chuckled. "It gets easier to get them into a routine as you have more kids, but if something is working, stick with it."

"Are Jared and Christian still trying to find a surrogate?" Anna snuggled into Gabriel's side as she asked the question.

"They've been looking. Since their surrogate couldn't carry to term last time, they've put the plans on hold. Although, Christian has been talking about adoption recently."

"They're such good dads." Tori leaned forward and put her water on the table.

"Hey, did you not bother to invite us?" Jade said as she, her husband Nic, Jewell, and Zane came in from the hall that led to the kitchen.

"Jewell, I thought you and Zane were working tonight?" Amanda twisted in her seat and waved everyone in.

"Nope. Ethan ran us out of the place. He wanted

to call his mom and dad on secure comms, and he told us he'd monitor the systems if something came through." Zane headed to the bar. "What do you want, babe?"

"Whiskey." Jade flopped into one of the oversized recliners.

"He wasn't asking you." Jewell dropped in front of the Christmas tree near Joseph and Ember.

"He's there at the bar, isn't he?" Jade drawled.

Nic reached down and grabbed Jade's hand, making her stand up, then he dropped into the chair and pulled her down on his lap. "Oh, I like this." She snuggled into his chest.

"Nic?"

Nic moved Jade a bit on his lap before answering, "I'll drink some of Jade's whiskey."

"Then make it a double," Jade quipped.

"Jewell?" Zane asked his wife.

"Juice?"

"There's apple, pineapple, or cranberry," Zane said as he stared at the fridge.

"Apple, please."

"Why are you drinking juice? Are you preggers?" Jade groaned. "For God's sake, tell me you're not."

Jewell shook her head. "Thinking about it, but no. If I get called into CCS during the night, I need to be ready to go." She accepted her juice from her husband. Zane delivered Jade and Nic's drink before he and his water bottle found a place on the floor by Jewell.

"I missed this at Thanksgiving," Tori said. The mood sobered as they all remembered why their annual gathering in November hadn't happened: Richard Berkley's orchestrated siege of Guardian. The man had kidnapped Faith and Tori, and Berkley's minion Amari had happily done a mind fuck on Tori. The lives that were lost during that battle weighed heavily on Frank's shoulders. Berkley had loved Frank's first wife, and she had loved Berkley. Only Frank found out about it far too late.

The room quieted. Tori leaned forward. "Dad, I know I don't have a right to ask this, but I'm going to anyway. Could you please tell me ... well, us ... I don't know, I guess the history that brought Richard Berkley to our door this spring?"

Amanda slowly turned her head to look up at him. He glanced down at her and then at his family gathered around the roaring fire and Christmas tree. The muted flashing of colored bulbs silently marked the time as his mind flashed back to days he thought were long forgotten. Richard Berkley. A ghost in his mind, but a very real and deadly physical force. Or he was until he was killed there on the ranch.

Frank gazed at his family, the ones tied to him by blood and the ones he'd claimed as his own. They were his legacy, the people who would move forward when his time on earth was over. He loved each of them and owed them what he knew about Elizabeth and Richard. Which was too damn little.

He nodded. "Every one of you has the right to know. You were brought into it. Makes it your business." He took a sip of his drink. "Where the hell do I start?" He shifted his gaze to Gabriel.

His friend lifted his drink and stared at the amber liquid. "At the beginning, my friend. At the beginning."

## 2

1979, *Coronado Naval Base, California, USA:*

"Mail call! A lot of people must miss your ugly mugs." Frank Marshall looked up from his bunk where he was cleaning his weapon. They'd made it back the previous night, and every last one of them had racked out past sunrise that morning. A rarity, for sure. Today was about getting ready to go back out again. As the squad's lieutenant, he broke tradition and bunked with his men. He didn't see a need for separation, and his team was one of the best.

Matchstick lugged the mail bag through the

door. They called him that because the little shit was as skinny as a toothpick but had a temper that flared as fast as a match. He was hell on wheels for being the runt of the team.

"Drago's got a care box from his mom!" Match yelled. Drago's mom sent cookies. Nothing special as far as taste went, but he shared them, and that made them special. Frank listened as more names were called. His mom and dad didn't do much writing. He sent them one letter a month and called when he could, letting them know he was still alive. Figured it was the least he could do since they'd encouraged him to leave the ranch and join the military. His pop figured he needed to see the world before he settled. No sense in always yearning and wondering what could have been.

"L.T., you got a letter." Frank jerked his head up. *A letter? For me?* That didn't bode well. He put the parts of his weapon on the bed just as the letter flew his way. He snatched it from the air and looked at the front. From his mother.

He put the envelope aside and finished putting his weapon together before he opened it. With his elbows on his knees, he read the words on the paper.

. . .

*FRANK,*

*We are okay, but I need to let you know that your Uncle Brent had a heart attack yesterday. He was saddling up old Slim and fell at the horse's hooves. Your pop found him. Old Slim was nudging him, trying to get him up. Your pop's not showing it, but he's concerned. The doc said if Brent makes it, he can't be ranching. We figured he could take over the paperwork from me. I can still ride fence and chase cows if the need arises.*

*I'm not telling you this to change anything. We're okay. The ranch is doing good, and we have hired two more hands. I promised to keep you up on what's happening, and that's what I've done. We read your letters time and again. I'm proud of you for getting out of here and seeing the world.*

*Love,*
*Mom*

FRANK DREW a deep breath and looked away from his mother's writing. Uncle Brent and his dad had run the Rocking M Ranch since their dad, his grandpa, had passed about twenty years ago. His Aunt Betty was just a young one when gramps died.

Fast forward twenty-some-odd years, and Brent was a widower. Found out too late his wife had the cancer. Nothing anyone could do for her except make her comfortable and mourn her. He glanced at the date on the postmark. It was marked three weeks before. *I'll call home tonight at dinnertime.* It would piss off Pop because no one interrupted dinner, but he knew he could reach them then.

"Want one?" Drago held his care package toward Frank.

Frank dipped in and took one of the larger pieces of cookie out of the box. "Thank you." He popped it into his mouth. Not bad.

"No problem." Drago nodded to the letter. "Bad news?"

Frank swallowed before he talked; unlike some of the men on the team, he still believed in manners. Guess that was drilled into his head by his folks, too. "Uncle had a heart attack three weeks ago. Not sure if he pulled through. I'll call today and find out."

Drago blinked at him. "They would have called the Red Cross, right? If he passed?"

Frank shrugged. "People in my neck of the woods tend to take care of business themselves. They wouldn't want to interfere with anything going on with me here."

"So, your old man is going to manage that big ol' ranch by himself?" Drago sat down on the cot opposite Frank. He picked up a piece of candy from the box and extended it to Frank. "Saltwater taffy. I can't stand the stuff, but my mom sends it every time."

Frank took the candy. "Thanks. They've hired hands, and he has my mom there. They'll manage."

"My mom would demand I come home and take over the business." Drago sighed. "I'm an heir to a dry-cleaning fortune." He laughed, adding, "If you consider two shops and a central laundry a fortune."

"Sounds like something you could make into a good living." Frank leaned back, resting his back against his wall. He opened the taffy and popped it in his mouth. The sweetness exploded across his tongue. It reminded him of that fluffy frosting his mom would make on special occasions. "Damn, Drago." He held up the little wax paper wrapper. "This is good."

"Yeah, you like it?" Drago's eyebrows popped up. "You're serious?"

"I do, and I am," Frank admitted.

"Here." Drago reached into the box and pulled out a plastic container of taffy. "I usually end up chucking it."

Frank took the candy. "Thanks. Have you seen

the lieutenant commander?" When they were on base, all communications with the team were done through Lieutenant Commander Paulson. A good guy by all accounts.

"He told Match he'd be back; he was called up to HQ." Drago flopped onto the bed, the box from his mom on his stomach. "I'd be okay with staying put for a few weeks. Getting tired of traveling."

"Not happening, Drago."

Frank turned to see Paulson standing at the door of their barracks. "Listen up. Everyone in the debriefing room in fifteen minutes."

There was a chorus of groans. Frank stood and set his shit straight. He grabbed his utility uniform blouse and buttoned it up before he picked up his garrison cap and placed his weapon in the rack. He headed out the door. As usual, the stampede of his team followed him.

Paulson met them at the debriefing room. Frank sat down and stared at the screen. A picture of Libya and Chad was shown from the overhead projector.

"Shit," Drago mumbled. "Gaddafi is at it again."

Frank nodded in agreement. He didn't doubt it. The man wanted not only Libya but Chad, too, and from what he'd seen in the news and heard during briefings, nothing this side of the grave was going to stop the guy.

Paulson flipped off the lights and closed the door. "This is a classified briefing. All information will be protected as such. Once again, we have military escalation in Libya. We knew the Kano Accord wasn't going to last."

His team made various comments under their breath. Frank didn't abide by talking back in that fashion. His pop would have cuffed him upside the head for mouthing off. He grunted his displeasure, and the team hushed up. He kept his trap shut and waited for Paulson to explain why they were there.

"Yesterday, the twenty-fifth of June, reconnaissance noticed a buildup of forces on the Libyan border of Chad. Today, approximately twenty-five hundred Libyan troops invaded through here." Paulson flipped the transparency, and arrows showed the location of the Libyan troops.

"Isn't that France's problem?" Toro, called such because he was a bull of a man, asked the question.

"We're not here to debate politics." Paulson flipped the transparency again. "You will be leaving for the nation of Chad at 03:00 hours tomorrow. There is a new civilian organization that will be working with you. They're a security firm that specializes in the retrieval of personnel from sticky situations."

"What, like kidnapped?" Joker asked and then laughed. The man couldn't talk without laughing. It was a nervous condition, but the guy was hell on wheels with a Kate. The best sharpshooter in the entire unit. Joker had read an article about the longest recorded sniper kill and slapped a scope on an M2 fifty-caliber just like the Marine sniper did in Vietnam. He'd spent countless hours honing his skill.

"Just like that but also in other ways. They call themselves Guardian Hostage Strike Teams. GHoST for short. The intent, if Guardian can get this off the ground floor, is to go in with a surgical strike and extract their target. Each team member has been trained in hostage negotiation techniques should the need arrive."

"Get in and get out with their person without getting killed," Blank added.

"Correct," Paulson acknowledged.

Frank turned and looked at Paulson when Ace asked, "Are they taking over underwater demolition, too?"

"No. We've been assured this company is primarily a humanitarian aid function, but these teams are made up of former SEALs, Rangers, Delta Force, and CIA members. All have been vetted and are in good standing. They can deploy not only overseas but in the United States, too."

"Bet that pisses off the FBI," Match snorted.

"A lot of turbulent waters in Washington right now. However, the concept has made a lot of the political types curious. Plus, the man directing the company has made a name for himself in Washington, and he has several congressmen backing him. Powerful allies, but the chairman of the Joint Chiefs of Staff wants to make sure these teams know what they're doing. They're civilian, well-funded, and acting in a private capacity for a governmental agency. Any questions?"

Frank cleared his throat.

"Lieutenant Marshall." Paulson acknowledged him.

"Which government?"

"Ours. We will be briefed on the mission when we land. Any other questions?"

"What are we going to be doing?" Drago leaned forward so he could see the L.T.

"You're going to be waiting and hoping the team doesn't fuck things up and need us to unfuck them. Any other questions?"

The silence in the room spoke for itself. "Get your gear cleaned and put together, and then rack out. Transport will pick us up at the barracks at 02:00 hours for an 03:00 flight. Dismissed. Lieutenant Marshall. A moment." Paulson pulled him aside and waited until Ace closed the door behind him. "The skipper has been asked to assign one person to this Guardian team as an observer. You've been selected. He wants a full report on capabilities, strengths, weaknesses, and the command and control. Your words will be fed straight to the Joint Chiefs of Staff. When you get back, you'll report to Naval Intelligence. They'll debrief you and send your report to the Joint Chiefs."

Frank took a moment to consume that flood of information before he spoke. "This Guardian team knows I'm coming with them?"

"They do." His superior nodded.

"All right. Blank will take control of the squad while I'm with the Guardian people unless you're appointing another?"

"Blank's your chief petty officer, but he can't make the call to go in after you should shit hit the fan. There is a lieutenant commander already in position in Chad. He's there as NATO observer, but he's a former SEAL. He won't go on the mission with the team if they need to deploy, but he will be the one to give the okay to move out. Good enough?"

Frank nodded. A new person inserted into his team would just fuck the flow up. If he were in trouble and needed his team to save his ass, he'd want Blank in charge. "I can live with that."

"Good. Get your squad ready. The skipper knows you're tired, but it can't be helped. Maybe someday we'll have more platoons in each of our teams. Rumor has it that the Joint Chiefs want four platoons on each team.

Frank cocked his head. "That would be almost five thousand people if you count support staff."

Paulson nodded. "Yeah, I don't see it either. Hell, we can't get a pay raise, and our enlisted with families are on welfare. Maybe someday in the future, the military will be seen as something other than a taxpayer burden. Just keep your eyes and ears open. The Skipper wants the bare-naked truth."

"He'll get it," Frank said as they walked out of the briefing room. He was damn good at watching people. If this civilian team was worthless, he'd call it fair. It was no skin off his nose one way or the other.

"The guy running this show is next door. I want you to meet him before you go overseas."

Paulson headed out the door, and Frank followed. They made quick work of moving from one building to the next. Paulson knocked on the SEAL team commander's door, and they were told to enter. Paulson opened the door and nodded for Frank to go through. "Not my show."

Frank nodded and entered the office. He reported in to the commander. "At ease, Marshall. I want you to meet Gabriel."

A man in a fancy suit and a shirt so damn white it would hurt your eyes stood up. "Lieutenant."

"Sir."

"Marshall is one of our best. I wanted you two to meet before we get involved in Libya or Chad."

"Can't say as I'm glad to have you with us, but I understand the rationale." Gabriel extended his hand.

Frank shook the man's hand, a firm handshake. "Can't say I'm too keen on being the third wheel, but I also understand the rationale."

Gabriel smiled. "I'll see you soon, then." He turned to the commander. "Sir, good day." Gabriel turned and left the office.

His commander waited for the door to shut before he turned to Frank. "Be careful over there. I don't need a civilian wannabe to cost me. Understood?"

"Completely, sir."

The man nodded. "Dismissed."

Frank did an about-face and headed back to the barracks. His gut told him Gabriel was solid. There was no give in the man, and even though he dressed in city-boy clothes, there was solid substance under that veneer.

# 3

*Present Day, Marshall Ranch, South Dakota:*

"GHoST Teams?" Jacob shot Gabriel a look. "I've never heard of GHoST Teams. What happened?"

Gabriel shrugged. "One of the many things that fell by the wayside as Guardian expanded. I wanted the GHoST Teams to be specialized and work hostage situations only. Remember, in that timeframe, there was a rash of hostage-taking. The first I remember vividly was the Munich Olympic Hostage Crisis. Then the Patty Hearst kidnapping in addition to numerous hostage and kidnapping events in

Europe. There were at least thirty cases in the United States that made national news. Countless others that didn't. It was needed."

"What happened when you called home before you went to Chad?" Amanda glanced up at Frank as she spoke.

He took a sip of his drink and continued …

*1979, Coronado Naval Base, California, USA:*

"Hello?" His mom's voice sent a wave of homesickness through him

Frank smiled as he looked out the glass of the phone booth. He had ten dollars' worth of dimes and quarters sitting on the small shelf in the corner for the call. "Hey, Ma. Tell Pop to stop frowning."

"Frank, are you all right?"

"I'm fine. Just got the letter you sent about Uncle Brent."

"Just now? The mail is slow to California."

"I just got back to the States." He couldn't tell them much, and they knew not to ask.

"Oh. Well, Brent is back at the ranch. He's got limitations, but he's going to take on the business end of the ranch. He and your dad are talking about buying two of the smaller ranches nearby."

Frank chuckled. "I take it you don't agree."

His mother grunted. He knew that sound. She didn't want to say anything to cross her husband, but she would let him know her displeasure with that sound. "What do I know? I'm only a woman."

"Hardly, Ma. You're his equal." It was the seventies, for God's sake. Women were more than wives and housekeepers. That idea was stupid. Capital-letter type of stupid. His mom and grandma had ridden round-ups, worked as hands, and done everything a man could do. Sometimes better than a man. Hell, there were women in the Navy, and they pulled their weight.

"Mention that equal thing to him sometime. Anyway, we're good. That contract we have for the cattle saved our butts last year when the market went down. They wanted to renegotiate, but we held them to it. Paid off."

"Sounds about right. I'm heading overseas again, but I wanted you to know I'm going to get out of the Navy at the end of this hitch."

"You are?" His mom sounded shocked, which didn't happen often.

"Yup. There have been some recruiters here from

the CIA. Figured I'd get out at eight like I told you and then work two years for them. That would put me back home in ten years like I promised."

There was a silence that held a moment longer than his liking before his mom cleared her throat. "You know, you don't have to come back."

Frank closed his eyes and sighed. "If I didn't, I might die. I needed this, as you and Dad said, but my blood is made up of Marshall land. It's where I'll raise a family and where I'll die. I'm coming home. That hasn't changed."

He could hear his mom sniff. "Here's your pop. Chuck, talk to your son."

Frank leaned against the back of the phone booth and crossed his combat boots.

His father's gruff voice came through the receiver, "You made your ma cry, son."

"Just told her I was coming home as we'd agreed. How's Brent, no horse dung surrounding it, Pop? I need to know so I can focus here."

"Not good. We called Betty, and she drove home from Vermillion. He pulled through, though, and the doctors said he could last another decade if he takes it easy. If he doesn't, his ticker is going to up and quit on him. He rests a lot, but he's got some good business ideas."

He heard his mom grunt, and he smiled. She was listening on the other phone. "Expanding while there's the money and the property is available isn't a bad idea. Land is money. And it's only getting scarcer." He'd seen the urban creep of San Diego. The city was building so fast. Where there had been fields when he was first stationed in Coronado, there were now strip malls and businesses and enough cars to strangle the freshness out of the air. It wasn't a pretty thing.

"My thoughts exactly," his father agreed.

"Then why in thunder haven't you said that?" his mom countered. Frank laughed and added four more quarters to extend his call. His folks loved each other deeply, but they were both stubborn and strong-willed.

"Lou, I *have* said that. Just not in those words."

"Frank, your father is getting senile."

Frank outright laughed. "I miss you both. Miss home."

"Come on back whenever you're ready, son," his father said before quickly adding, "We've got everything covered here."

"You'd tell me if you didn't?" He listened to silence for a heartbeat.

"Yes," his dad said at the same time as his mom.

That's what he loved about his folks. They believed honesty was the only policy, not the best policy.

"I'm traveling back overseas tomorrow. Don't know how long I'll be gone."

"Just promise me you're keeping your head and butt down," his pop groused.

"Flat to the ground," he promised.

"Good. What about a vacation this year? Probably forgot how to ride a horse by now." His mom got the question in. She always did.

"I'll be home for calving. Hopefully. Depends on what the Navy has in store." He'd made it home four times for calving season. He'd like to think all the running and training the SEALs had him doing kept him fit. Fat chance. When he was done wrestling cows for thirty days, he was sore in places that shouldn't have muscles. Not that he'd tell anyone that.

"Can we send you anything?" His mom always asked that at the end of their calls. He reached into his pocket and pulled out a piece of that taffy Drago had given him.

"Ma, do you think you can find any saltwater taffy?"

"I'm sure I could. Why? You develop a sweet tooth?"

"In fact, I think I have." He popped another piece of taffy into his mouth and carefully folded the little wax square, putting it into his pocket. The Navy liked to think they'd taught him how to police after himself, but the fact was his ma would clock him if he littered or made a mess and didn't clean it up. He was more afraid of her than the Navy. That was saying something. The Navy had weapons.

"Be on the lookout for a package, then."

"I will be. Love you both." He made sure they knew. His wasn't a nine-to-five job.

"Love you, too," his pop and ma took turns saying.

"Bye." Frank waited for them to hang up before he put the receiver down and collected his change. He needed to get back to the barracks, make sure his team was ready, and rack out for a couple of hours.

*1979, Libya, Northern Africa:*

FRANK WATCHED Gabriel walk up to him as they crouched and moved away from the helicopter that dropped them onto Libyan soil. "Our intel tells us we need to move south. Your liaison will bring you into

Chad. I have to get my men moved. I'll see you in Djedda."

Frank grunted and narrowed his eyes as the man jogged across the tarmac and got into a beat-to-shit jeep.

"Marshall?" a UN officer called to him. Frank turned on his heel and hustled to the man.

"That's me." His eyes were everywhere. Being in Libya was reason to be careful.

"Come with me. I'll take you to your liaison."

Frank motioned to his men, and they filed after the UN officer. The fucking mission had started out for shit, but that happened at times.

"Barracks are on the left. Food is down here and to the right. Showers over there." The heavy French accent of the adjutant from the 1 REC pointed out the low house that was to be their temporary quarters. The 1 REC and the 2 REP were French divisions that had taken control of two Chadian towns. Frank gazed over the portion of Djedda that he could see. He wasn't one to judge, but he was certain the town had seen better days. Several buildings were bombed out, and it lacked civilians.

Lieutenant Commander Morgan, the NATO liaison who met his squad and escorted them into

Chad, nodded. "Thank you. We are to meet Guardian forces here."

"Oui. They are here." The adjutant indicated a small building next to their barracks.

Frank turned. "Listen up. Bunk, chow, showers." The rest of the team looked as he pointed. "You've got one hour."

Ace extended an arm to him. "Give me your bag, L.T. I'll claim you a rack."

Frank surrendered his go-bag. "Thanks. Tell Blank to get everyone fed."

"Roger that," Ace acknowledged. Frank turned and headed after Morgan, who was making a direct line to the Guardian quarters.

Morgan knocked on the door. The thing swung open to the business end of an M-16.

Frank's 16 swung on its sling, and if the bastard shot Morgan, he'd get a 5.56 through the gut. The click of Frank thumbing his weapon to fire was loud and clear. The big blond fucker's eyes shifted to Frank.

"Craig, enough with the hostilities. If they were going to kill us, would they knock?" A tall man with dark black hair and a square chin elbowed past the tank of a man at the door. Frank studied both men. Gabriel was obviously well-educated. He could tell by the way he spoke. The man with the weapon? That one was like a bull his pop had once had, all rage and power with no mind for how either was spent. He was one Frank would keep an eye on.

"I'm looking for Mr. Gabriel." Morgan's eyes stayed on the man with the weapon. Smart move.

"That would be me. Craig, drop the aggression."

The man sucked his teeth and dropped the muzzle of the M-16. When he spun, Frank noticed the weapon was still on "Safe." So, a stupid, rage-filled bull. Great. What in the hell was he getting himself into?

"Come in." Gabriel stepped aside. Frank walked in behind Morgan. The hut was clean, and there was a stack of packs against one wall. "I'm sorry, I missed your name." Gabriel was talking to Morgan, so Frank kept his mouth shut.

"Lieutenant Commander Morgan. This is Lieutenant Marshall. He's the SEAL who'll be accompanying you. His team is here for backup should it be needed."

"It won't be." The blond bull sat down on a bench.

Frank cocked his head and narrowed his eyes. The stupid bull didn't play well with others. How had he made it onto a team? What skill did the man have that was needed?

"Nice to see you again, Marshall." Gabriel totally disregarded his man's words. He turned to Frank. "We're leaving in three hours. Can you be ready?"

"I'm ready now." He was fucking tired and hungry, but he'd been tired and hungry before. "What is the objective?"

"We're going about four hundred and thirty kilometers north and east to N'Djamena. Our objective is to extricate a man and, if it is still intact, the experimental equipment he built that was left when the FROLINAT was defeated in June." The coalition forces were fractured everywhere from Frank's understanding. Gabriel pointed to the location on a map spread out on the table and held down by a rock on each corner.

"What type of equipment?" Frank kept half his attention on the bull in the corner of the room.

Gabriel stood and looked at Morgan. "I'll tell him because he's now part of my team. You're not."

Morgan rolled his eyes. "I'm out of here, then. Your team knows the score?" He directed the comment to Frank.

"Yes, sir." Blank would defer to Morgan should the need arise. If it didn't, the boys would laze around and eat French chow for ... Frank looked at Gabriel. "How long will we be out?"

"Four days." Gabriel turned his gaze to Morgan. "On day five, if we aren't back, we aren't coming back without help."

PRESENT DAY, *Marshall Ranch, South Dakota:*

"WHO WAS THE STUPID BULL?" Jade's voice yanked Frank from his memories.

"Craig McNair." Gabriel's voice held a bitterness. "A friend. Until he wasn't." Gabriel pulled Anna closer to him.

Jacob glanced at his watch. "Don't start again until I get back. I need to bring down the presents."

Frank looked at the clock on the wall. "Getting late. We can pick this back up tomorrow."

Tori leaned forward. "Daddy, I know you're an intensely private man. I don't want you to—"

"Needs to be told. But not tonight. After the children wear themselves out tomorrow, we'll get back together after dinner, and I'll finish."

"We can have the older ones watch all of them except the babies," Faith suggested.

Amanda nodded. "We can find something for them to do."

Frank finished his drink as the kids wandered back to their rooms to retrieve presents. Amanda and Anna went with them, leaving Joseph, Jason, Gabriel, and himself.

"Craig." Gabriel shook his head. "He almost cost me everything."

"How so?" Joseph asked from the floor where he was still lying.

"Craig was a close friend. He had my back when we were in the CIA together. What I didn't see was that he loved me. Back then, being gay wasn't talked about. He assaulted Anna, kept things from me, and when she disappeared, he made sure I didn't know. She was pregnant with Gabrielle at the time. It took far too long to find her and my daughter."

Jason shifted in his chair. "How did you find out he was in love with you?"

"He was killed overseas. A vicious assignment. One of the last I went on. I found documents on him that told me what he'd done." Gabriel downed his Pappy and stood up. "I need another unless we're actually done dragging up bones for the night."

"I'm done. We'll finish tomorrow." It was after that mission with Gabriel that Frank met Elizabeth for the first time. Actually, it was because of the mission.

Frank stood. "I'll see you all in the morning." Christmas morning came early, especially with little ones in the house.

"Night," Joseph and Jason said in unison.

Gabriel followed him out of the room to the kitchen. "Probably shouldn't go too much into the mission."

"Won't." Frank rinsed out his glass and extended his hand for Gabriel's. "That little nuclear suitcase is still buried deep, right?"

"As far as I know. A dirty bomb on steroids. Thank God Gaddafi or the insurgents didn't know what they had." Gabriel leaned against the counter. "When I think of all the dumb luck we had during that mission ... Lord, I didn't know enough to know I didn't know enough." His friend chuckled.

"None of us did. The concept started Guardian's overseas efforts, though. A damn good thing." He wiped his hands off as he spoke.

"Wasn't what I envisioned originally." Gabriel rubbed the back of his neck.

"Know it. Ever think of revisiting that? Now would be the time." Frank had thought about it over the years. He had some ideas. Old and antiquated, but the young ones would be able to take the ideas and run with them.

"I've thought about it. But I'm not sure if one more rod in the fire is what we need right now." Gabriel stared sightlessly across the room.

Frank grunted, the exact sound his mom made when she disagreed with his dad but wouldn't say the words.

Gabriel blinked and then laughed. "All right, all right, my friend, we'll talk about it after you finish telling the kids how Berkley came to your doorstep."

"Sounds about right." Frank cuffed Gabriel on the shoulder, and they both headed upstairs.

# 4

*Present Day, Marshall Ranch, South Dakota:*

Tori took her meds and drank the entire bottle of water. The medications made her mouth dry all the time, but at least the panic attacks and anxiety were manageable. She still hadn't gone into her dad's study. She couldn't face seeing it again. Yes, it had been rebuilt. Mentally, she knew that, but emotionally, she was still in that room at times. The study was where Amari had convinced her that Jacob and her boys were dead. That room was where she'd lost hope and had been broken.

"You okay?"

She jumped and turned at Jacob's question. "Yeah, sorry. Just thinking."

He nodded and smiled at her. God, he'd been so patient with her. "The presents are all downstairs. The boys are sleeping. Talon is snoring like a freight train."

"He, Reece, Lizzy, and Kadey spent the day riding." She remembered doing the same thing growing up.

"And here I thought Talon didn't like horses," Jacob quipped before he started to brush his teeth.

"He likes Kadey, and he tolerates his cousin Lizzy because he likes Kadey." Tori laughed at her husband's frothy-mouthed expression.

"No way." Jacob drooled toothpaste when he spoke and dipped down to spit out the remainder. He rinsed his mouth quickly. "You think so?"

Tori rolled her eyes. "Boys. You're clueless." She walked out of the room and pulled the blankets down on the king-size bed.

"No, we're not. Well, not all the time." Jacob stripped down to his boxers and got into bed with her. She turned toward him. He leaned in and kissed her chastely. "Good night."

She put her hand on his chest, stopping him from rolling over. "Jacob, can we talk?"

He stalled. His entire body was immediately alert. "What's wrong?"

"Nothing. It's just ... God, this is so awkward." She flopped onto her back.

"Babe, just say it. I'm here." He stared at her, and her eyes filled with tears. He'd suffered as much as she had, hadn't he? "What? What is it?" He cupped her face with his big hand.

She turned back to him. "I want us to make love."

He blinked and recoiled a few inches before his eyes narrowed. His voice cracked with emotion as he asked, "Are you sure?" The first time they'd tried after the attack, she'd had a panic attack and ended up in the corner of the closet, freaking out. That was almost four months ago, in September. She missed the intimacy, his touch. Her meds had been adjusted twice since then, and she'd worked with Jeremiah about the "why's" of that attack. It had nothing to do with Jacob, and yet it had shattered a precious piece of their relationship. Now, it was time to piece those shards together. To make them stronger than they'd been.

"Yes." She reached to his chest and put her hand over his heart. "I'm positive."

Jacob made quick work of divesting himself of his boxers. Her nightgown was up and over her head just as quickly. He stared at her. His eyes traveled up and down her body before he lowered his head and swept his lips across hers. She chased him, but he moved away before he returned, giving her small kisses, almost-there touches, and drawing away as if her husband, who knew her better than anyone in the world, was testing how fast or far he could push her before she lost it again. She cupped his neck and pulled him down, separating his lips with her tongue. Those big, muscular arms went around her, and she wrapped her arms around his neck.

She knew his body as well as she knew her own. His muscles played under her touch; the feel of his skin on hers soothed an ache deep inside her. The rasp of his chest hair against her breasts was familiar and sensual. She wanted all of the sensations, all of the familiar, the feelings, the love.

Tori had to break the kiss to breathe. Panting, Jacob looked down at her. "Are you okay?"

"Fine, need to breathe." She smiled up at him, and that's when the smile spread across his face. The one that told her that her man wanted her. It was reserved for her and her alone. "Make love to me, Jacob. I need you."

They'd been through so much. So many highs and lows punctuated the opus they'd created through their life together. He stared at her and whispered, "I'd wait forever if you needed me to."

A tear slid from her eye and trailed to her ear. He bent down and caught it with his tongue. She hugged him tight and whispered, "I know." Because she did know it. That man had given her life when they'd first met. He was her constant, her north star. Her life aligned around and through him.

He covered her, keeping his weight on his elbows, and centered his long, hot cock at her core. But he didn't enter her. No, that wasn't his way. He made love to her body with his lips and hands. His mouth teased and tormented as his hands explored and excited. When he finally entered her, she lifted her hips and helped him seat himself deep inside her. They kissed as he began to thrust. Her hands shook, but not due to anxiety. No, this time, her body shook on the brink of release. Jacob rose to his knees and pulled her up into his lap. He lifted her, and she helped guide his cock into her again. She dropped her head back and groaned as he hilted himself deep within her. She lifted as he withdrew, and they came together again. She arched her back and dropped her arms to the bed behind her.

Jacob's hand traveled up her stomach between her breasts to cup her neck. His hips pumped as he held her steady. She could feel her breasts moving up and down, and he thrust into her. Obviously, Jacob noticed, too. His free hand traveled to one, thumbing his nail across the hard nipple. He gave the same attention to the other. She felt her insides tightening. She needed this release. Needed them to be *them* again. Jacob's free hand traveled down to her clit. He massaged her just hard enough. *Perfect. Yes. God.* Her body tightened and then rippled a current of incredible sensations through her.

She grabbed his shoulders, and he brought her back up as he pounded into her, chasing his release. She didn't know how long it took for him to climax. Her world was still fractured from the climax he'd given her.

He held her as she lay on his shoulder, gasping for air. A shudder ran through him, and she smiled against his neck. "I love you."

He laid them both down and stared at her. "You are my world."

"I'm trying to be better." She wiped at the sweat that beaded across his forehead, damping his hair that was now sprinkled lightly with gray.

"You are perfect the way you are." He dropped a

kiss on her lips. "I love you as you are, strong yet fragile, vulnerable, beautiful, loving, scared, and completely mine. Get better for you. I'll be here every step of the way. I'll catch you when you fall and cheer you on when you succeed. Forever."

∼

JEWELL STRETCHED as she exited the bathroom. They'd taken quarters living in the underground facility. She'd stayed in them before, both at the ranch and the Rose, the training facility in Arizona that Joseph controlled. The underground rooms were like Lycos' mountain cave, but she preferred the cave. There was a natural element that metal walls lacked.

Zane lay under the blankets on the bed. She made her way over and slid on top of him. She wore his T-shirt and nothing else. It was her favorite nightgown. Well, *their* favorite. She picked a new one each night. "Merry Christmas," she whispered before dropping a kiss on his lips.

"Is it midnight?" Zane asked.

Jewell snuck a look at the clock on the other nightstand. "On the East Coast, yes."

"Then I can give you your present."

"Yours is under the tree." She frowned at him. "Mine is, too. I saw the box with the big silver ribbon."

He chuckled. "This is something I wanted to give you in private." He reached down, rolling, so she almost fell off the bed. He grabbed her and continued to fish under the bed. Finally, he pulled out a small box. "This is for both of us."

"What is it?" She sat up, straddling his lap.

His hand traveled up her thigh, resting under his T-shirt. "Open it and see."

She ripped off the bow, and the ribbon floated to the bed. Easing the cover off the box, she stared at ... a rock. She picked it up and examined it before she held it up to the light, trying to see if there was something special about it. Finally, she shook her head. "Okay, I give up. Why did you give me a rock?"

"It's symbolic. I actually gave you a mountain."

Jewell stared at her husband. Most of the time, he was the one who made sense of the rest of the world for her. But right then, he wasn't. She looked at the rock and then at him. "A mountain."

He nodded and smiled. "Put it together, babe. Who has a mountain?"

"Lycos," she answered immediately. "What does his mountain have to do with this rock?"

Zane took the rock from her. "Symbolic. I bought you a mountain."

"Why?" She really had no idea what to do with a mountain or the darn rock. Which was symbolic. Jewell shook her head. "I still have no idea what you're talking about.

"I bought you a mountain where we can live."

Jewell narrowed her eyes. "We're living here until Guardian is set up again."

"Unless we can set up another node."

"On the mountain."

"Yes."

"That's crazy. Unless we had a place like Lycos', it would take years to build and hide a node."

"We do."

"We do what?" She sighed. She hated it when people tried to explain things to her and they didn't link with anything her mind could grasp. "I don't understand. I'm sorry."

Zane smiled at her. "I'm not doing a good enough job explaining it, then. I bought Lycos' mountain. He didn't want it after so many people had been there. He and Bethanie are working on a new one far, far away."

Jewell jerked back and looked at the rock. "It would be just us?"

"Yes," Zane acknowledged. "No one would know where you're working. We have Jillian's power cells, so we're off the grid."

"I wouldn't have to go back to an office building." Her hands began to shake. She hadn't told anyone how afraid she was of being in a big building again. Her heart hammered even when she walked into her apartment building.

"No. I've talked at length with Gabriel and Jason. CCS nodes will be the new normal. All of them will back up to servers at the Rose."

"Because no one knows where it is."

"Exactly. And no one will know where the other nodes are."

"We'd need several in the states. One in Australia, England, perhaps other countries." She held the rock and turned it in her hand as she thought about the possibilities. "Ethan could run one. I could train more."

"Three of our team have requested to come back to work. They'll need to be cleared by the docs, but we'll get them up and running and assign each a node as they develop if they're up to the task. If not, we'll find jobs for them. Until we sort that, they can work out of our apartment. Lycos set up his old office and safe room with the equipment I sent him.

You'll have to tweak it and make sure it's sufficient for your needs. I was guessing based on what we did to the apartment."

"The Rose will need a redundant storage facility. Just in case. I don't want to be caught with our data britches down again."

Zane laughed and took the rock from her. He set it on the bedside table. "Gabriel ordered two more yottabyte servers. One for our mountain. One for the Rose."

"God, I love it when you talk data to me." She pulled off his T-shirt and flung it across the room. "You know it gets me hot."

Zane tipped her over and rolled on top of her, tangling them in the sheet and blanket that had covered him. He kissed her neck. "You okay with moving to the mountain?" he asked as his lips made their way down to her shoulder.

"Yes. Two conditions." She gasped when he took her nipple into his mouth.

He didn't answer for a long time. When he finally lifted away, he asked, "What are they?"

*What?* "Huh?" She grabbed his hair and tried to move him back to where he was.

He lifted against her protests and smiled. "Two conditions to living in the mountain."

"Oh." She fisted his hair and smiled. "Pizza oven."

He lifted over her body. "Already installed."

"Excellent." She shifted her hips and rotated against his cock, which was stiff and separated from her by sheets and blankets. She tugged at the material. "Stupid sheets."

His head dropped for another kiss. "What was the second condition?"

She stopped tugging on the cotton and thought for a minute. "I can't remember, but it was important. Rain check?"

"Deal."

Jewell tugged hard at the same time Zane lifted his hips. Her hand grasping the sheets flew up and hit her in the nose, and a brilliant blast of pain burst across her face. "Oww!"

Zane was beside her in a heartbeat. "Babe, oh shit. Are you okay?"

"No. I think I broke my own nose." Her voice was muffled behind her cupped hands. She could feel her nose bleeding. The warmth oozed toward her hand. She kept her hands cupped. "Bathroom."

Zane helped her into the bathroom, the light turning on as they walked through the door. She made it to the sink before she released her hands.

Yup. Damn it. A wet washcloth was placed under her nose. "I'll call Doc and have him come down."

"No!" Jewell said, but the washcloth muffled her. "It's Christmas. I just have a bloody nose." She glanced up at the mirror. And maybe black eyes, but she wasn't going to say that to Zane.

"Babe, I'm so sorry."

She turned to look at him while pinching her nose to stem the bleeding. "Why? You didn't hit me. I hit me." Zane blinked and then smiled. The smile turned into a chuckle and then a belly laugh. She narrowed her eyes at him. "Why are you laughing?"

"Because you are the most amazing, wonderful woman I've ever met." He pushed her hair out of her face. "Let me look." She cautiously removed the washcloth, but it started bleeding again. "Okay, put that back on and tip your head back a bit."

"Is it broken?"

"No, it doesn't look like it."

She relaxed in relief. "Thank goodness."

"Let's get you cleaned up. We'll call Doc if it doesn't stop soon. Okay?"

She nodded and shoved her head back again. "I remembered the second condition."

"Yeah, what's that?" Zane used another washcloth to remove the blood that dripped to her neck and chest.

"I want a wolf or a fire-breathing dragon or maybe an attack cat, so when you leave me alone on that mountain to go to town or whatever, I'll have protection." She and Bethanie had talked when she was last at the mountain, and the wolves made Bethanie feel safer when Lycos was away.

Zane barked out a laugh. "I'm not sure I can find a dragon or an attack cat. Is that a thing?"

She opened one eye. "A tiger or mountain lion, maybe?"

Zane blinked and then laughed as he shook his head. "I'm not sure that's doable."

Damn it, having a tiger would be really cool. She sighed. "Then I want a wolf to protect me when you're not home."

Zane put down the washcloth and wrapped his arms around her. "I'll do my best. Has it stopped bleeding?"

She took the washcloth away from her face. "Yeah. I think so."

"Good. Into bed with you." She reached for him, and he stepped back. "No, to sleep. We'll talk data tomorrow night."

"Or in the morning before we go to the big

house?" Jewell turned and made sure to sway her hips on the way to the bed. She heard the growl behind her and smiled. She was getting sex in the morning. She already had her tiger, didn't she?

∽

JARED HUNG up his and Christian's coats before he hustled to the stairs. Marcus was dead to the world. He and Chloe, Jared's sister Jasmine's oldest child, had played until they literally dropped. Christian carried their son up the stairs in front of him. His husband's wide shoulders, narrow waist, fantastic ass, and thick thighs were on display, and damn it, he wanted to tackle the man. Children first, then adult needs.

A growl formed deep in his chest. "Shhh," Jared said quietly.

Christian turned to look down the stairs at Jared. "I didn't say anything."

"I was shushing myself," Jared replied.

Christian stopped and turned on the stairs. His long, thick blond hair fell from his shoulder and swung along the breadth of his back. Jared sent his eyes up and down his man's body again. Fuck, Jared wanted to bury his face in the man's hair while he devoured his husband.

Christian waited until Jared lifted his face, then looked at him and lifted an eyebrow. "What?"

Jared leaned forward and whispered, "I'm going to fuck you into oblivion."

He saw the shiver that went through his husband. "Don't make promises you don't plan on keeping."

"I never do." Jared leaned forward and took the lobe of Christian's ear into his mouth, nibbling it. Christian dipped above him, and Jared grabbed him, steadying his husband and child.

Christian tugged his ear from Jared's mouth. "I'll meet you in our bedroom."

Jared shook his head and took Marcus. "I'll put him down. You go. I'll meet you in the shower." Jared took their son.

Christian leaned forward and kissed Marcus before he met Jared's eyes. "Five minutes."

Jared nodded and watched his husband bolt up the stairs and jog down the hallway. He shifted his son's weight in his arms and followed at a slower pace. Life had a tendency to get in the way of their personal time. It had been scarce since the Siege. He'd been working from home, but as time moved on, his work hours had extended and extended. Marcus and Christian developed their own routine outside the house so he could work. It was the best and worst of outcomes. The best because he and his family survived the collapse of the building. The worst because the effort to keep things running, modify procedures, and find new ways to obtain information, along with the process of reconstructing evidence for cases going to trial, had proven difficult and sometimes impossible. Now that CCS was fully functioning, they had access to the information, but the backlog for Jewell and Ethan to process was so large it defied any type of reality. Even if they had fifteen data analysts working at full tilt, it would still take years to find a new normal. They had two. Three more would come back at the new year.

He pushed open Marcus' door and laid the boy down on the bed. His son. That was something he would never have believed would happen. Christian had made that possible. His husband was literally the wind beneath his wings. With care, he took off Marcus' coat, hat, and snow boots. He tugged off his jeans but left him in his T-shirt. If his son woke up now, getting him back to sleep would be next to impossible. He was so excited about Christmas.

*Crap.* Christmas. He had presents to get downstairs. He pulled the covers over the little guy and made his way to the connecting door, which led to his and Christian's room. Jared tiptoed across the room and opened the closet door. The presents were neatly stacked. He pulled them out and made a quick run downstairs. The tree was huge, but there were presents everywhere. It was what happened with their family. So many nephews, nieces, brothers, and sisters to buy for. Even though they all agreed on a price cap for presents, it was a massive Christmas that made him feel a bit guilty in its magnitude. He placed the Santa presents and bolted back up the stairs.

Jared checked on Marcus one more time before he started stripping. Jeans, shirt, socks, and boxers went flying as he crossed the room. He opened the bathroom door and swallowed his fucking tongue.

Christian stood in the shower. His head tipped back as the water sluiced down his muscled body. Jared opened the door and stepped into the shower. Christian looked over his shoulder, and his eyes dropped down Jared's body. "You took longer than five minutes."

"I had to take the presents downstairs."

Christian turned and grabbed him by the waist, jerking him closer. "Make it up to me."

Jared grabbed Christian's hair and devoured his husband's mouth. They fought for dominance, and he fucking loved the challenge. His husband's strength was a powerful aphrodisiac. He reached down and took both of their cocks in his hand. The water helped lubricate the slide of his hand as he gripped them both. Christian bucked into his hand as their tongues fought for supremacy. Jared clenched his husband to him and felt the air leave Christian's lungs. Only then did his man concede and lean into him. Jared broke the kiss and fed on Christian's neck as his hand kept stroking both of them. Christian's grip on his biceps bit as his blunt nails dug into Jared's skin.

Jared lifted his head and stared at the man he loved more than life itself. "Are you ready for me?"

Christian's eyes opened, and he nodded. "Fuck me to oblivion."

Jared spun his husband and reached for the lube they kept in the shower. He slicked up and used two fingers to start opening his man.

Christian reached back and grabbed his hip. "Now."

Jared dropped the lube on the soap shelf and

placed his cock at Christian's entrance. He grabbed Christian's neck and lifted him up and against his chest. "I love you," he growled as he pushed inside. Christian's hand moved to his cock, but Jared grabbed his arm. "Just from me." He thrust in and out of his man until he found the right location.

"Jared," Christian shouted and slapped his hands onto Jared's thighs. He held Christian still, all his strength, his mind, and his body working in concert to nail his husband's prostate and make Christian climax before the tight heat and utter bliss of his husband's body forced him to reach down and stroke Christian to completion.

The feel of his husband's muscles contracting around and against him and the sounds coming from Christian drove him into a sexual frenzy.

"More. Fuck, more, Jared. I need more." Christian's words begged for permission.

"You need me. Say it." Jared pounded into his husband.

"Only you. God, only you." Christian's hands tightened on his thighs.

Jared bit down on Christian's shoulder, and his husband sucked in a surprised gasp seconds before he felt his husband clench around him. He opened his eyes and watched as Christian came. Jared reached down and stroked his man as he melted into Jared's thrusts. He chased his orgasm and threw himself over the cliff, falling into his release.

Their loud pants and the fall of the shower floated back around them. Jared held his husband in his arms, the water surrounding them, keeping them in a blanket of togetherness. "I love you," Jared whispered in Christian's ear.

Christian turned his head so it was under Jared's chin. "You are my world. Don't ever leave me."

Jared moved and turned his husband to face him. "Leave you? I couldn't exist without you. What would make you say such a thing?" He searched his husband's eyes for any clue.

Christian sighed and leaned into him. "There hasn't been much of this, of 'us time' lately. Sometimes I ... worry."

Jared lifted Christian's chin to make his husband look at him. "I've neglected you." Christian shook his head and tried to look down, but Jared wasn't having it. "I have. I'm sorry. I'll do better. You are my world. You and Marcus are everything to me. Never doubt that. We'll make time for us. Make time for this. I miss us as much as you do." He leaned down and kissed his husband. This time the kiss wasn't contested; it was soft, gentle, and full of the love he had for this man.

When the kiss ended, Christian dropped his head to Jared's chest. "I know you're busy."

Christian leaned against him, and Jared wrapped him in his arms. "There's too much work and not enough hours, but I'm going to put a stop to the insane schedule. Restructuring Guardian has to include a better way forward for Dom Ops. Even with Nic and Jade carrying part of the burden, the workload is too much." He shifted Christian to the wall and picked up the soap. He'd been neglecting his husband. That had to change. Starting now.

# 5

*Present Day, Marshall Ranch, South Dakota:*

THE DAY HAD BEEN full of fun, laughter, and food. Unfortunately, a piece of Frank had been on edge, tense, and dreading the coming conversation. It was in part that he hated talking ill about Elizabeth. He'd steadfastly refused to do so in front of the girls. But tonight, he'd tell his truth and pray it wouldn't taint his girls against their mother. Well, any more than those letters she'd written had done. They were a stain that had directly caused untold damage to him and his family.

Amanda brought in a tray of eggnog, and so did Anna. Each had three large pitchers on their tray, leaded for the ones who consumed alcohol and unleaded for those who didn't. There were several trays of finger foods, and his entire family was sitting in his living room. Chairs from the den had been dragged in. There was laughter and horseplay going on. He sat on the couch and accepted a spiked glass of eggnog, holding Amanda's cup as she sat beside him.

Gabriel and Anna were once again beside them, and their adult children were sprawled around the room. The teenagers were watching the younger ones, and the monitors by Faith and Joy were focused on the newest members attending Christmas at the Marshall ranch.

Jared was on the floor leaning against the wall by the fireplace, Christian between his legs. Next to them were Chad and Jasmine. Joseph and Ember and Drake and Jillian were in similar positions against the other wall. Mike and Taty were in front of the fireplace. Thankfully, the fire had died down a bit, or they'd be roasted quickly. The rest were spread among the couches and chairs to include Deacon, Ronan, and Gabrielle.

Frank waited for Amanda and Anna to have a

seat. It seemed to be some silent cue from the heavens. His family all stopped talking and, as one, looked at him. He grunted, causing a spattering of laughter. "Everyone caught up on events?" He looked at Mike, Jared, and Jasmine. They nodded. He turned his gaze to his boys, Dixon and Drake, and Gabriel's kids. Everyone went north and south with the head wags. Seemed the kids had been talking.

Tori took a sip of her drink before she spoke. "You were heading into Chad to observe Gabriel's GHoST team."

"I did that." Frank nodded. "The details are classified, but suffice to say, Gabriel and his men were equipped to handle what they needed to handle."

"Classified? After all this time?" Jewell asked from Zane's lap.

Frank narrowed his eyes and leaned forward. "Do you have black eyes?"

Jewell snorted. "I do. I was pulling the blankets that were pinned under him, and he moved. My fist came up, and I clocked my nose. I had a bloody nose, but I got a mountain out of the deal."

Jacob choked on his eggnog. Jared and Christian laughed outright, and Dixon and Drake nearly busted their guts laughing.

"What? What did I say?" Jewell's eyes darted around the room.

"Nothing, babe. Your brothers are grade-schoolers." Zane rolled his eyes. "Get your minds out of the gutter, jerks. I bought us Lycos' mountain. We both have issues with going back into big facilities right now. He has the power and satellite equipment already installed."

"I get a wolf, too. I already have a tiger." She waggled her eyebrows, and all the women laughed.

"Wait, they can laugh, but we can't?" Jacob lifted his hands. "What the hell?"

Gabriel leaned over to Frank. "You going to grab control of this?"

Frank shook his head. "They'll figure it out sooner or later." He hoped.

Tori lifted her fingers to her mouth and gave a long, sharp whistle, quieting the room. "I want to hear the rest of the story." She leveled her gaze on her husband.

Jacob's eyes popped open. "It wasn't me!"

A thunder of feet from above sounded. Talon, Tristan, Trace, and Tanner sprinted into the living room. "What's up?"

Tori blinked at her boys and then laughed.

"Nothing. Sorry, I wasn't calling you. I was getting everyone's attention down here."

"Oh, cool." Talon smiled, walked past the food spread, picked up a tray, and all four boys sprinted out of the room.

"I gave them their own food." Amanda looked shocked as the boys ran up the stairs, laughing like loons.

"Teenage boys. It's probably gone," Faith chuckled. "They were waiting for a reason to come downstairs and get more."

"Okay, so, on with the mission. How can it still be classified? I thought the only things that remained classified that long were … Oh." Tori's eyebrows lifted. "Gaddafi had a nuke?"

"We can neither confirm nor deny that information." Gabriel smiled as he spoke.

"Holy shit." Joseph sat up from his reclined position. "How?"

"If I were to speculate …" Frank picked up his cup. "I'd think of something like a modern-day dirty bomb, only with a more powerful detonation and half-life."

"Probably something like that." Gabriel nodded. "Not that we could speculate."

"No. Couldn't. Wouldn't be right," Frank agreed.

"So, how good was Dad's team?" Ronan asked before he popped a cracker into his mouth.

Frank chuckled. "Damn good, or they would be when he made some tweaks to the personnel who made up the team."

*1979, Chad, Central Africa:*

"Why in the hell can't we just drive straight in, find what we're looking for, and leave? We have the armament and the backing if shit gets real."

Frank rolled his eyes and stared at Gabriel's right-hand man. McNair was a piece of work. The man always found something to bitch about. That comparison between his dad's livestock and McNair hit the bull's eye, and there wasn't any pun intended on that one. "Because there are factions out there that will fire on a vehicle instead of allowing it to go through their territory no matter who is in it or what backing they have. Do you want to get blown up, or would you find something to bitch about then, too?" Frank shouldn't have said a word, but he'd had it up to his eyeballs with the man.

Gabriel laughed and elbowed Craig. "He has you pegged. I like him."

McNair's lip lifted in a sneer. "So, tell me, Mr. Hot Shot SEAL, what would you do if you were in charge of this mission from this point forward?"

Frank reached into his pocket and grabbed two candies by mistake. He handed one to Gabriel and unwrapped one for himself. He'd be damned if he'd share with McNair. He popped the candy into his mouth and crossed his arms, staring out into the Chadian landscape. "Jump in north of the location. We wouldn't have to go farther than the foothills of the Tibesti Mountains. We can come back in from the north. No one will be looking for insurgents from that direction due to the Libyan forces on the Chadian border."

Gabriel turned to look at him. "Lieutenant Marshall, that is an excellent idea."

"We'd need a plane and someone stupid enough to fly over that area. They do have anti-aircraft armament, you know," McNair sneered, dismissing him.

"They won't pick us up if we go in on a helicopter and stay below five hundred feet."

"They'll hear us," McNair countered.

"But they won't know where we are or where we're going. Yes, we'd have to watch our six, but it would give the team a chance to reach the target area, retrieve the person and item you're looking for." He'd seen the area they were trying to reach on the map and compared it to the topographical makeup of the country. The clans that had carved up the northern territory didn't play well together, so there was little chance of reinforcements arriving if shit got real.

"Exit strategy?" Gabriel's eyes narrowed as he gave Frank all of his attention.

"Assign a location to the northwest for a copter to pick us up. They hold as long as they can. If we don't make it, we head east into Niger and then call for air support to get us the hell out of Dodge."

Gabriel turned to Craig. "Told you."

Frank narrowed his gaze and switched his focus from Gabriel to McNair. The guy shrugged. "So, he's smart. I'll give you that."

Frank took another piece of candy out of his pocket and unfolded the wax paper. "Why do I feel like I've been played?"

Gabriel turned back to him. "What would you do if you were told you had an unknown thrown into your team? You'd test him, feel out his abilities and sensibilities, true?"

Frank chewed on his taffy for a bit. He nodded. "I would. What are your entrance and exit strategies?"

Gabriel nodded to the hooch they were assigned. "Come with me, and I'll show you." McNair fell into step beside them, and they made their way back to the quarters. Gabriel spread out another map that showed a different location than originally marked. "This is the true location of the asset and his item. He's gotten word out that he'll be here at eleven tonight. We need to be there waiting for him. We're using black ultralights launched from this location." He tapped the foothills of the Tibesti Mountains.

Frank lifted from the map. "Slow-moving and can be heard. How are you getting the man out?"

"We have a dual ultralight with two motors for the exit. We stop here and go in on foot. Any drone of the ultralights wouldn't reach the settlement here." Gabriel's fingers traced the route to the camp where the primary said he'd be waiting.

Frank considered the information before he nodded. "All right." He'd never flown an ultralight before, but he figured if a bull-like McNair could make it happen, he'd have a better than average chance of handling it.

*Present Day, Marshall Ranch, South Dakota:*

"Holy shit. We have to get some ultralights. That would be so much fun." Drake sat up and slapped Dixon's leg.

"No," Chief said emphatically.

"Come on, man! Could you imagine the—" Dixon leaned forward and started.

"No." Amanda stood up and reached for the eggnog pitcher. "You have enough toys. Anyone else?"

There were takers all around. Frank took a refill and a Christmas cookie.

"Did you get the guy?" Jacob asked before he popped a cracker with cheese on it into his mouth.

"We did. Without a shot fired." Gabriel nodded. "I had a lot of grand ideas back then." He chuckled. "But nothing compared to what we've been able to build."

"And we're going through a transformation again." Jason lifted his unleaded eggnog. "Thankfully, you've provided us the foundation to pivot and make changes to become a better organization than we were before the attack."

Gabriel nodded. "Since we have all of you in one

location, we'll meet tomorrow after lunch and go through the anticipated foundation and structure. We're going to modify and simplify, giving you support and staffing to handle the organization. I know all of you have worked since the attack without a day off. We'll recruit and maintain the highest quality staff. I've brought Rio North on board to begin that process."

Jared nodded. "Rio has connections with all the spec ops personnel."

"He does, but he also has connections to get us support personnel from those spec ops teams. People with clearances, with the technical skills to hit the ground running for CCS, and for all other administrative duties. We aren't recruiting outside the spec ops fields until we're at one hundred percent."

"What about the Operator?" Jewell asked as she sat down with a plate of cookies and sweets.

"Operator Two-Seven-Four didn't sustain the loss most of our sections did. The duty location will be classified like the Rose, and protection will be worked the same way we'll protect the nodes for CCS. We're waiting for the equipment to be built and installed. We should be back at full capacity by May of next year."

"It sure has changed since your original inception of the organization," Deacon spoke softly. He didn't talk much, but when he did, people tended to listen. He was a born leader.

Frank took a drink of his eggnog and pulled a piece of taffy from his pocket. He'd forgo any other sweets. He liked what he liked.

"It has. I have folders of my original concept for Guardian. Hell, even the reorganization we were doing for the Thorn Teams is now a moot point, or it is until we can stabilize missions and decentralize our vital infrastructure."

"The original concept and this mission Uncle Frank was talking about was before you met Mom, right?" Gabrielle asked. Gabriel's oldest was a beautiful woman with Gabriel's coloring and Anna's grace. She also had a top-secret clearance, as did her brothers. Hell, even Chad had a clearance. Being a part of the family made it mandatory.

"Several years before, yes." Gabriel nodded and smiled at his wife. "Your mom was still rocking her scrubs in Colorado then."

"Gawd, Dad," Ronan groaned. "I can't unhear that."

"Mind bleach," Zane snorted.

"Excuse me?" Ronan asked.

"Ethan says not even mind bleach can get the visions out of his head," Jewell explained.

"I don't want to know *why* he said that, do I?" Jason asked.

"Probably not," Zane chuckled.

"Frank, you met Elizabeth shortly after that mission, right?" Amanda said from across the room where she was refilling some cups with eggnog.

He nodded.

Elizabeth.

That was the portion of the story he'd been dreading.

# 6

1979, *Coronado Naval Base, California, USA:*

"Naval Intelligence." The driver stopped in front of the building and announced their location like Frank didn't have a clue. He sighed and got out of the car that had been sent for him. He could have just walked across base. Though it seemed like a waste of gasoline and effort, he thanked the seaman who'd been dispatched to bring him to the principal's office. He was told to come straight to the building once he'd returned to base. Well, his team was the priority. He made sure they were bedded down and then checked in with his chain of command. Last time he'd checked, he didn't work for Naval Intelligence. An oxymoron, if ever there was one.

Frank stretched. He was tired, jetlagged, and hungry. He'd even run out of taffy somewhere over the Atlantic, and that in and of itself was a point of contention. He'd come to love those little bursts of sweet throughout the day. Even if he had to scrape the candy off the wax paper with his teeth when it melted in the Chadian desert. So to say he was in a foul mood was an understatement.

He walked through the door and up to the one and only desk in the entryway. The Petty Officer Third Class who ignored him didn't help his mood. Not one bit. Now he knew he was twisted tight, so he counted to ten before he barked at the guy. He needed to be fair, but common courtesy had a time limit. If you couldn't lift your head to meet someone as they entered your building, well, then you got what you got. "Seaman!"

The petty officer damn near jumped off his seat. Then he made a mistake. He sat up straight and opened his mouth. "That's petty officer, sir."

Frank leaned down, planted both hands on the *seaman's* gray metal desk, and growled. "I don't care if you're the Admiral of the Navy or Chesty Puller himself. When someone comes in that door, you do your job and greet them."

"Is there a problem here?"

Frank heard the woman's question, but his eyes didn't budge from the face of the flushed and sweating seaman in front of him. "No," he growled to whoever was trying to save the young petty officer from shitting himself.

"Are you Lieutenant Marshall? The commander has been waiting for you."

He lifted an eyebrow as the petty officer's eyes drifted down to his name tag. Frank watched the kid's Adam's apple bob hard. "Do we have an understanding of our duties, *seaman*?" Frank quietly asked the man, never once blinking.

"Yes, sir." The man's whispered reply was for him only. He glared at the man and slowly lifted his hands off the desk.

He turned around and stopped short. *Holy hell.* The blonde woman was either poured into her uniform or sewed into it because it was molded to her every curve, and brother, she had a lot of them.

She smiled. "I'm Ensign Frazier, the intelligence specialist assigned to your current mission. I'll take you to the commander's office. He'd like to speak to you, and then we'll do our debrief and type up that report for the Joint Chiefs of Staff." She talked as she walked, and it was everything Frank could do to focus on her words and not the sway of her hips. She was a right punch to the gut and uppercut with the left type of knockout all rolled into one.

He shook his head. It had to be the jet lag. He'd never fixated on a woman like that before. He was tired. Too damn tired. That had to be it. Nothing that a good week of sleep couldn't set right. Hell, his ma would have slapped him into next week if she'd caught him ogling a woman's backside that way. Where the hell was his mind?

She looked over her shoulder, and her brows drew together. "Lieutenant Marshall?"

He blinked and lifted his eyes to meet hers. "I'm sorry, what?"

She gave him a half-hearted smile as if she knew where he'd been looking. And didn't that make him feel like a horned toad? She repeated her question. "I asked if you wanted coffee."

"Yes, ma'am. I'm sorely going to need some. I'm dead tired." He scrubbed his face.

The smile was a little more genuine that time. "I wish we could allow you the time to rest, but this information is headed to the highest level." She turned down another corridor, and he followed. "The commander's office is through there. I'm next door here." She pointed to the door. "When you're finished, come in. I'll have coffee."

"Thanks." Frank nodded and knocked on the door to the commander's office. The talk was short and sweet. Frank was out the door and knocking on the ensign's door not more than four minutes later.

"Come in," her voice called out, and he opened the door.

"Lieutenant Marshall." She motioned her hand to the seat in front of her desk. "I didn't know how you took your coffee. There's cream and sugar on the bookshelf if you need it."

His eyes cut to the little cups and packets. "No, thank you." He'd never liked all the frou-frou stuff in his coffee. His ma and pop loved it, though. Even got some creamer that was pre-made and stored in the fridge. His dad about had a fit over that at first. They had milk cows for cream; spending money on it was stupid, or so he'd said. Until he tried it. Frank sat down and took the mug she'd indicated. "No, thank you. Black is fine."

"Good. Shall we start the debrief, Lieutenant?"

Frank took a sip of his coffee. It was hot, bitter, and strong enough to strip varnish. It was perfect.

"Going to be a long morning if you keep calling me Lieutenant Marshall. My name's Frank."

The ensign blinked and then smiled. "Elizabeth."

Frank took another drink.

"So, what I need first is for you to tell me what transpired and your observations of the team in question. I'll transcribe it shorthand, and then I'll ask specific questions relating to the questions we're getting from the Joint Chiefs. Once it's done, I'll type up the report, you'll review it, and then sign it unless we need to make changes."

It took four cups of coffee and a hell of a lot of yawning to get through the transcription process. By the time he finished reading the report she'd typed up, the words were blurring, but she'd done a great job of taking his words and making a proper report.

"And with that, you can go." Elizabeth took her pen and the papers back as Frank handed them to her.

Frank cleared his throat. "I owe you an apology."

Elizabeth's blonde brows rose in question. "About what?"

"Earlier in the hall. I don't know why I acted that way. I'm a better man than that." For some reason, he didn't want this woman to think he was a cad.

She smiled and cocked her head. "Then you should make it up to me. Dinner. Tomorrow night."

Frank blinked and waited for his tired brain to catch up with his jetlagged understanding. "A date?"

She chuckled. "You're seriously tired, aren't you?"

"Ma'am, I haven't slept more than a handful of hours in the last five days." He was beyond tired.

"Yes, Frank, a date." She bent down and scribbled something on a scratch piece of paper. "My address. Pick me up at six-thirty tomorrow. My number is below it if you need to adjust the date or time."

Frank took the paper and folded it, placing it in his pocket. "I look forward to it."

She smiled at him, a brilliant and happy smile. "So do I. Go get some sleep, Frank. You're dead on your feet."

"That I am." He nodded and turned to leave.

"Frank?" He stopped and looked back at her. "You're the first man ever to apologize. There aren't many gentlemen in the service, especially in the officer ranks."

He made a tsk sound. "Which is a sad commentary, isn't it? I'll try to make up for their faults."

Elizabeth laughed. The musical sound bounced

around the room. "You've already started. I'll see you tomorrow."

He nodded and exited her office. Dog tired and muddle-brained, he felt lighter than he had in weeks.

~

FRANK SLEPT like the dead for a full eight hours before he made his way to a candy store in San Diego. He bought way too much saltwater taffy and a small box of chocolates to take to Elizabeth. Then he stopped at a florist and picked up a long-stemmed white rose with yellow tips on the petals. It reminded him of Elizabeth's hair, pale and beautiful.

He pulled up to her apartment building in his truck. His cowboy boots were shined, and his jeans pressed. He'd never wear the clothes his men wore. Wide-legged trousers, silk shirts, and wide lapels on jackets weren't his style. He wore a button-down shirt, his best jeans, belt, boots, and a cowboy hat. If Elizabeth didn't like him for who he was, then he'd take her to dinner and say goodbye when he brought her home.

Frank took the stairs two at a time and knocked on her door. She opened it up and damned if what he saw didn't stop his thoughts dead in his tracks. She was wearing a gold satin outfit. Slacks and a top with a droopy ... no, cowl neck. The material molded to her body, and her tan skin looked like it was glowing against the color of the fabric.

"Wow. You look nice." He rolled his eyes and then laughed at himself. "And let me introduce you to my teenaged self. Mr. Smooth Moves."

Elizabeth's hair fell over her shoulder as she reached for the flower and small box of chocolates. "Thank you, Mr. Smooth Moves." She chuckled when he groaned. "Come in. I just need to get my shawl and put this in a vase."

"You have a nice place." He looked around at the tiny apartment. There were no family pictures, but the apartment was decorated nicely.

"Thank you. Someday I'm going to have a grand house with a view. I want to see forever from the windows and have enough room that I'm not cramped in the slightest." She poured water into a frosted white vase and set the rose in the long flute. Elizabeth grabbed a matching strip of cloth and draped it over her shoulders. "I'm ready." She picked up her purse and smiled at him.

"I have reservations at The Marine Room in La Jolla." It was about a half-hour's drive, but he figured they could visit. The place was pricey, but he'd been there once before and liked how the wood bar curved into the room and the waves actually pounded on the glass during high tide. It was a controlled fury that reminded him of the massive thunderstorms that rolled through South Dakota, something you were in awe of and pulled toward no matter the danger.

"That sounds lovely." He let her lock her door, and they made the trip to La Jolla. The conversation on the way was relaxed and fun. Elizabeth was smart and funny.

After they were seated, Elizabeth leaned forward and whispered, "Petty Officer Preston wanted to file a complaint against you." Frank grunted. Elizabeth tipped her head back and laughed. "That sound needed no explanation. I believe you just flipped off the young man, didn't you?"

Frank couldn't hide the smile that pulled on his lips. "That sounds about right." He ordered a whiskey for himself; Elizabeth ordered a chardonnay. "Tell me about your family." He figured that was a safe topic.

"Ah, well, my parents lived in New York. My dad was a stockbroker who was a bit too imaginative in his dealings. He was arrested for insider trading.

He's still serving his sentence. My mom, bless her, was ravaged by the press and the people who lost money in my father's deals when the SEC intervened. One night, she took too many pills and chased them with vodka. She never woke up."

Frank shook his head. "I'm sorry. I didn't know."

Elizabeth leaned forward. "It's okay, Frank. I don't hide it. I'm very upfront about my folks. They screwed up, but I didn't. I was already in college. No one knew I was related to the infamous Crandall Frazier. I graduated and applied for a commission in the Navy. I revealed everything in my clearance paperwork. I didn't want anything to stop my advancement or be questioned. Honesty is always the best policy. My father should have remembered what he taught me. So, tell me about your family."

Frank took a sip of his whiskey. "My folks run a ranch in South Dakota. They're hardworking, salt-of-the-earth type folks."

"Do you have a lot of land?" Elizabeth asked as the salads arrived.

"We do, and it looks like my father is in favor of buying more." He assumed his dad and uncle would carry on with the purchase of the two smaller ranches. It made good sense.

"What do you do on a farm?" she asked before she took a bite of her rabbit food.

"Ranch. Farmers grow crops, ranchers raise livestock," he corrected her. It was automatic.

She snapped her eyes up to him and laughed. "I'm sorry. I didn't mean to insult you."

"You didn't. I'm not a farmer." He shrugged. He didn't play in the dirt. The closest he came to that was digging water wells and cutting hay for winter. "A typical day is up at five, head out, and do the morning chores. Feed horses, calves if it's the season, chickens, hogs, whatever you have. Then back to the house for breakfast. The cattle are checked. We maintain countless miles of fence line. Make sure the herd is healthy, keep the water flowing, and stop the herds from overgrazing the land. Most of that's done on the back of a horse. We don't usually eat lunch. Dinner is at six-thirty sharp. Then you do the nighttime chores and go to bed. Start over the next day."

Elizabeth put down her fork, barely having touched her salad. "You enjoy this kind of life?"

"I do," he admitted. Hell, he was homesick for the routine and the rhythm of that life.

"Why are you in the military? A SEAL on top of

that?" She carefully wiped the corners of her mouth with her cloth napkin.

"My parents. They didn't want me to regret taking over the ranch. They told me after college that they wanted me to go out into the world. Do whatever I wanted for a while." He shrugged.

"And going through the hardest training in the world seemed like a good thing to you?" Elizabeth smiled at him.

"Seemed to me if I was going to do something, I'd give it my all. I'm leaving the SEALs, though." He said it out loud for the first time, and his throat didn't tighten at all. He was pretty impressed with how okay he was with his decision.

"What are you going to do?" She nodded when the waiter asked if she was done with her salad.

"I've applied to join the CIA. I'll do that for a couple of years before I head home." He wanted the experience.

"Wow, but you know what, I get that. I really do. I have another three years on my commission, but I want to get to D.C., and I want to get into the CIA or the FBI. I love working with tidbits of information and making the puzzle fit. Anything that stimulates my mind is kind of like cocaine to me. That hit of sensation when a key fits a lock and it opens is euphoric."

Frank leaned in. "Sounds like you know a lot about how cocaine works."

Elizabeth threw back her head and laughed, making all the men in the establishment look. He puffed up a bit at that knowledge. Elizabeth was a live wire, and she sparked that certain something that made her desirable. "Frank, I really like you." She laid her hand over his. "Don't ever change. For anyone." He grunted, and she laughed again. "See? That's what I mean. You're an individual, and you're cool with that. So many men want to be what everyone else is, do what they're doing. I don't see that in you."

Frank took another drink and leaned back as his steak came out. Elizabeth's smaller plate of shrimp and pasta looked interesting but not enough to swap out beef. "Been raised to be who I am. Don't know any different, and I don't conform to societal pressures."

"That is exactly why I like you, Frank Marshall. You're a man of principle, aren't you?"

"I try to be." He wasn't a saint. Not by a long shot. But he knew the difference between right and wrong.

. . .

*Present Day, Marshall Ranch, South Dakota:*

"So, our mom asked you out?" Tori stood and reached for a plate to put some food on.

Jacob got up and put his eggnog cup on the tray. "I'm hitting the hard stuff. Anyone else?"

There was a huge shift in people as they stretched and moved for food or drinks. Frank answered Tori. "She did. We had five, maybe six dates before she was transferred and I got out."

"Anything serious?" Keelee asked.

Frank considered how honestly to answer that question. They were intimate, but they both knew it was a temporary thing. Elizabeth had her sights on promotion and working in D.C. He was within six months of leaving and joining the CIA. There was an attraction between them but no emotion that would prevent them from going their own ways. "Yes, and no." He'd leave it at that.

Tori snorted. "The modern-day way to say that is 'It's complicated'."

Frank grunted. "Wasn't. Just wasn't in the cards for us. She wanted a career and advancement in Washington. I wanted to see what else was out in the world." They'd parted as friends who'd been occasional lovers.

"Frank, you want a real drink?" Gabriel asked as he lifted off the couch.

Frank nodded. "Thank you." He glanced at the clock and sighed. He'd hoped a hell of a lot more time had ticked off the clock, but then again, he owed his family this conversation.

"Do you want me to leave so it'll be a little easier to talk about Elizabeth?" Amanda whispered to him.

He turned his head to stare at his wife. "I never loved her the way I love you. Never, not for a second. I thought what we had was good and we could make a go of it. We got married because of Keelee, and we tried. Divorce wasn't an option for me. I did my best to make a good life for her."

Amanda lifted a hand to his cheek. "I love you, Frank Marshall." He leaned down and kissed her.

"Awww ... that is so cute." Jade's comment broke them apart. "I want to be sexually active when I reach your age."

"Jade!"

"What the hell?"

"Oh, my God!" A chorus of comments from their adult children rang out.

"What? You guys are so hiding your head in the

sand. Don't you think they let their freak flag fly? I swear, a bunch of ostriches." Jade flopped onto the couch next to Nic. Her husband just shook his head, put his arm around her, pulled her close, and whispered something in her ear. Jade laughed and turned her face up for a kiss. Obviously, Nic was down for a little senior sex, too.

Frank chuckled and took a sip of the Pappy that Gabriel had poured him. He still enjoyed sex, and so did his wife. He was old, not dead. Hell, if he didn't look at the mirror, sometimes he'd forget he was more gray than not. His body was still strong, and his mind was sharp. His eyes, on the other hand, needed help when he wanted to read, and his hands had a bit of the arthritis in them, but all in all, he was glad to be alive and healthy.

# 7

Present day, Marshall Ranch, South Dakota:

"But you left San Diego, right?" Keelee asked as she sat down with a plate of finger food and a glass of red wine, not Anna's cold stuff.

"I did. I got out of the SEALs at the end of my commission, and I joined the CIA. Because of my training with the SEALs, after initial training, I was sent to Bolivia. Operation Condor." Frank glanced over at Gabriel as he sat down with a drink for himself and Anna.

"What a messed-up situation." Gabriel sighed and shook his head.

"Why? What was Operation Condor?" Ronan asked.

Frank sighed and lifted his glass, looking through the tawny color of the liquor. "Operation Condor was essentially government-sanctioned killings of hundreds of thousands of Latin American civilians as the governments in the southern cone of South America banded together to try to wipe out Marxism."

"Was that a real threat?" Jewell made a noise, and Zane tapped her back with his hand. She swallowed hard. "Was it?"

Frank filled his lungs and sighed. "You have to remember, at that time, there was a strong anti-communist sentiment throughout the world. Cuba had been saber-rattling and forced the Bay of Pigs issue. The southern cone of countries used that sentiment to plan assassinations of politicians and prominent figures. They did it all through a communications system called CONDORTEL."

"Is that like Ma Bell?" Jade quipped.

"It was more like a direct line of communications from one leader to the next. The thing is, the United States installed it in the Panama Canal Zone, and it was reported that South American intelligence personnel used it to keep in touch with each other."

"So, the US supported this operation. The tone of your voice tells me that it wasn't a good thing," Zane asked.

Gabriel shook his head. "We thought it was originally. We traveled to Bolivia on the government's behalf. That's where we found out the facts."

Frank nodded. "It was my last mission for the CIA. When I got out of Bolivia, I traveled to D.C. and put in my resignation. It took a while to get approved. Six months, to be exact." The CIA hadn't been pleased that his sense of morality required him to resign, but he wouldn't be a part of what was happening in South America. He knew he couldn't say anything about what he'd seen, but he didn't need to. Gabriel would do more than he ever could, and he left that ball in his friend's court.

"What were you two doing in Bolivia?" Jason asked.

"I was on the security team for people setting up computerized lines between the intelligence community and the Condor community." Frank shook his head. "I didn't know at first about the operation, but I learned afterward. Mass graves, people going missing. Political assassinations, prison camps where people were taken in the middle of the night and never returned. I didn't find out until later how deep the CIA was involved with the training and torture tactics, among other things, until I came back to the States. That's when I accepted the job Gabriel offered me in Bolivia."

"What did you do in Bolivia? You had to have found out what was happening?" Deacon asked.

Gabriel cleared his throat. "I, too, found out about Operation Condor after I arrived in Bolivia. I talked to Frank when we met up in the foothills of the Andes. I knew him from our time in Chad, and it didn't sit well with me that he was working on an operation that could cause further harm. So I told him what I knew, what my plans were, and suggested he start digging. I offered him a job. Figured he'd come to the same conclusion as I had."

"I told you I couldn't give you more than a year." Frank lifted his glass.

Gabriel chuckled. "Many times. It was my goal to keep you so happy you'd never leave."

"No chance. I was always heading back here." Frank took a sip of his liquor.

Gabriel nodded. "I never lost track of you after that. Even after you and Elizabeth got married."

Frank nodded.

"Wait, what happened in Bolivia?" Nic asked right before Jade popped a cracker into his mouth.

Frank looked over at Gabriel, and the man took over the explanation. "I used our family money and connections to systematically dismantle the ability of those nations to persist in the endeavors. I also applied pressure to make sure the US Government moved away from its catastrophic-leaning 'if we don't see it, the atrocities don't happen' policies. Movement of that level takes years, but it worked."

"So, you two saw each other in Bolivia?" Ronan asked as he lifted his drink to his lips.

Frank nodded. "We did. Briefly. I was heading out; he was heading in." They'd met at a joint camp. Frank looked at the fireplace. It was a hell of a night.

*1980, The foothills of Nevado Sajama, Bolivia:*

HE'D GROWN up around mountains. The Black Hills of South Dakota, the Rockies in Colorado. He'd seen some high points in his life, but the Andes Mountains were something to behold. He adjusted his pack and thanked God they were on the way down instead of up. Up had been a hell of a climb. The altitude of the site his technicians were working at made breathing difficult. Kind of like breathing through a straw. Thank God he was in shape. The technicians didn't fare as well, and they had to limit the physical exertion of each day's trek. But they were done; the communications system was installed, and he was heading back down the mountain. Back to the United States. It couldn't have happened soon enough for him.

The base camp was active, which was unusual. Frank was working point, so he hunkered down and watched for a moment. He reached into his pocket and pulled out a piece of the sweet confection. His eyes stayed on the camp as he unwound the wax paper and popped it in his mouth.

"Fuck." He swore under his breath. It was becoming a habit, one he'd have to break when he headed home, but seeing the bull of a man in the center of the camp was not what he wanted tonight. He'd prefer his sleeping bag and someone else keeping watch over his ass. Three weeks up and down the mountain had made him irritable. He was on his second-to-last piece of taffy, and he'd packed double what he'd thought he'd need.

He tracked another person coming up to the fire. Ah, well, the bull's wrangler was there, too. Frank stood and looked over his shoulder. The technicians were a bedraggled bunch. The other two CIA agents and local militia that accompanied them looked like they'd been ridden hard and put up wet. Not a pretty sight.

He waited until he was seen by his crew and then stepped out of the wood line and headed for the camp. He saw when Gabriel noticed him. A smile spread across his face. "Lieutenant Marshall, your military commanders won't like that beard you're growing."

"Left the Navy. Working for the Agency now." He grasped the hand that was offered. "Thinking twice about that decision."

"Mr. Hot Shot. How's it hanging?"

Craig McNair extended his hand. Frank narrowed his eyes at the man. "None of your business. I see you're still attached to his hip." Frank tossed his head in Gabriel's direction. He didn't like the guy. At all. He'd be civil, but he wasn't going to shake the man's hand.

McNair dropped his hand and sneered at Frank. "Still too good for us?"

Frank shook his head. "Not at all. Just honest with myself. Always have been, always will be."

"Craig, make sure our stuff is stowed and our

team is taken care of, will you?" Gabriel's comment was an order, not a request. The bull snorted something, but he left. "I want to talk to you. I'll give you time to clean up and eat, but we're leaving at first light, and there's some shit you need to know." Gabriel's tone was deadly serious.

Frank glanced at his watch. "Twenty minutes. My tent." He nodded to a tent far away from camp and the fire.

Gabriel nodded. "I'll be there."

Frank made haste in making sure his team was all in. He left his M-16 in the weapons rack under guard and grabbed a change of clothes. The water supply was ample thanks to a small river. He showered in cold water and grabbed a C-Rations kit. He was inside his tent eating when Gabriel pushed the flap open.

"Smells better around you now." Gabriel sat down and pulled out a small flask. "Care for a little?" He unscrewed the top. Frank shook his head. He was on a mission.

Gabriel winked and returned the flask to his shirt. Frank swallowed the food in his mouth. "Testing me again?"

"Maybe." Gabriel leaned forward. "I've recently discovered some concerning information."

Frank set the box of food aside and leaned forward. "Spill it."

And Gabriel did. For the next thirty minutes, he detailed shit that set Frank's hair on edge.

"Can you prove any of it?" Frank finally asked after Gabriel finished.

"I can. You don't have to believe me, but damn it, I know you're good people. You don't need to be caught up in this shit because the blame will run downhill. Fast."

Frank nodded. He could see that, especially in a politically stratified organization like the CIA. "I'll have to do my own checking. I'm heading back to the States."

"When you find out it's true, what will you do?"

"Leave, go home."

"You could come to work for me. I need help expanding Guardian Security. There's an immense need for what we're doing here and even more for humanitarian aid to countries torn by war and political strife. I want to make a difference, to bring light into the darkness."

Frank reached into his bag that he'd left in camp and fished around for his refill of taffy. He pulled the bag out, opened it, and offered Gabriel a piece. While he thought of the correct words to say, he chewed on the sweet. "I liked the concept of the GHoST teams."

"Which I haven't had a chance to get off the ground other than that one mission. There's such demand now for private intervention in situations such as these." Gabriel unwrapped his candy. "I'd let you pick your job. I can teach you what you need to know, but I can't teach what you have."

Frank grunted. "And what's that?"

"Morality, integrity, loyalty, responsibility." Gabriel stared at him as he answered. "Think about it. This is my card. My number. If this isn't what you signed up for, I'll hire you in a heartbeat."

Gabriel had always been a straight shooter with him. He couldn't think of a single reason for the man to lie about what was happening. The problem might be getting anyone to corroborate what he had told him. Frank took the card and looked at the number engraved on the heavy paper. No name, nothing but the number. "If it does come to this, I couldn't work for you for more than a year or so. I'm heading back to South Dakota then."

"I'll take you for as long as you'll work for me."

*Present Day, Marshall Ranch, South Dakota:*

. . .

"You found out he was telling the truth." Amanda made the statement, and both Frank and Gabriel nodded.

Frank sighed, "It wasn't hard because it wasn't being hidden. The administration at the time was ignoring our involvement. Left a bad taste in my mouth. That communications shack on that mountain was temporary. Fueled by batteries that needed to be replaced continuously, but it was part of the network that was being used for terrorist activities." Frank nodded.

"What happened then?" Jewell asked. She was leaning against Zane, and his arm was draped around her possessively. Frank scanned the room. All of his boys were caretakers and protectors.

"I put in my resignation. The suits weren't happy. I was shuffled between administrative jobs until my paperwork was processed. That's when I met your mom again."

**8**

*1980, Washington D.C.:*

"Frank? Frank Marshall?"

Frank spun from the bar where he was having a drink, his Friday night tradition in Washington. He smiled and stood up. "Elizabeth. You made it to D.C." He kissed her cheek as she leaned in.

"I did. Unfortunately."

That didn't sound good. He looked around. "Are you with someone?"

She shook her head. "No. I'm not with anyone."

And that sounded even worse. "Care to tell me about it?"

She blinked and looked up at him, a smile forming on the edges of her lips. "You know what? I don't want to talk about it, but I'd love to have a drink with you and catch up."

"That sounds about right." Frank looked around the crowded bar. "I don't see a table."

"I live not too far away. Come over to my place, and I'll buy you a drink." She tucked her hand around his bicep. "I swear I thought it was you, but Frank Marshall wearing a suit sans cowboy boots and a bolo tie, well, my mind couldn't put two and two together."

He dropped a five on the bar, which would cover his drink and the bartender's tip. "Dress code." He rolled his eyes before he covered her hand with his and led her out of the bar.

"Dress code? Ah, you're working with the Agency." She nodded. Outside, the air was brisk, and she shivered. Frank took off his suit jacket and placed it over her shoulders. "Thank you. I missed this. You always treated me like a lady."

His head snapped toward her. "You mean someone hasn't?"

She sighed and shook her head. "It seems my

father's past has come back to bite me in the rear." She gave a sad chuckle. "Bloodlines are everything."

Frank grunted. "For cows and horses, yes. For people? That's a load of horse dung."

Elizabeth laughed. "I missed you, Frank. You were always so good for my soul."

"Good to know." He dropped his arm over her shoulder, and they walked down the street together in silence.

She pointed across the street to a newly constructed building. "This is me." He opened the door, and they entered through a spacious entryway. The marble floor screamed money, and so did the dark wood accents. She called the elevator and produced a key. She inserted the key and hit the top button. The elevator jerked them heavenward.

"Top floor?" He cocked his head at her.

"Yes. I'm staying in a friend's apartment. I could never afford this."

The door opened, and they walked out of the elevator into her living room, but it was the view that caught and held his attention. "That's some view." He moved to the floor-to-ceiling windows and took in the vast expanse of the Washington skyline.

She moved up beside him. "You can see for miles."

"Just what you wanted." He smiled at her. She'd wanted that view. The one she hadn't had in San Diego.

She headed toward the bar in the corner of the room. "I thought it was. Sometimes when you get what you want, the thing you're looking for tends to slip through your fingers."

"Not as great as you assumed?" He walked over to the bar and took the crystal tumbler of amber liquid. "Thank you."

"You're welcome. No, what I had for a while was perfect, but I guess some things just aren't meant to be." She took a sip of her Chardonnay. "Are you stationed here in D.C.?"

"For a short while. I'm leaving the Agency and joining Guardian." He and Gabriel had confirmed his move to Guardian, and the CIA couldn't hold him up for much longer. His supervisor said a week or so last week, so he should be free of the government job in the coming days.

"Guardian. There is a lot of hush-hush talk about them. The brass is concerned they're forming their own mercenary forces. Please have a seat."

They sat down, and he took a sip of his drink. "Guardian is going to be big someday. Very big. I've met the man running it. Right now, he's scrambling to keep up with the growth and expansion." He put his drink on a coaster on the table beside him. "I'm hoping to be part of helping him map out that effort." They'd had several long telephone conversations and two dinners when Gabriel was in town. The man worked more than anyone he'd ever met, and that was saying something because work was a twenty-four-hour-a-day thing where he came from.

"I'm confused. Aren't you going back to your farm?"

He chuckled and corrected her again. She loved to tease him about the ranch. "Ranch, and yes. I'll go back. That land has been in my family for as long as anyone can recollect."

"I'd love to see it someday." Elizabeth sighed and shook her head. "If it wasn't for the Navy, I don't know what I'd be doing right now."

"Still love the job?"

"I do," she wagged her head back and forth, "but the glow has diminished. As much as I wanted a career, supporting someone in a relationship doesn't sound half bad." She laughed. "I may have changed my priorities."

"Sounds like you had a total shift." He nodded. "I'm happy you've finally found a path."

Elizabeth shook her head. "I found the path, and then the cliff tumbled from under me."

"Care to talk about it?" he offered again. "You had a bad breakup?"

She nodded and drank almost all of her wine. "We're completely over. It was hard to face at first, but life doesn't always give us what we want." She turned toward him. "Sometimes, it gives you what you need." She leaned forward and kissed him.

Frank pulled away. "I don't want to take advantage of you, Elizabeth. If you're pining over someone ..."

"He's out of my life forever. I'd like you to make love to me, Frank. Make me feel beautiful and cherished. Make me feel alive here." She took his hand and placed it over his heart.

He left the next morning. Elizabeth had been wild for attention, and he'd tried to satisfy that need. Tried so hard one of the condoms he had with him had ripped while they were in the act. She swore there was no need to worry. He wasn't sure what she meant by that, but he wasn't going to make a mountain out of a molehill until there was a need to do so.

The CIA let him go on Monday. By Tuesday, he'd finished in-processing at Guardian Headquarters. Gabriel showed him the plans for the new building, the hardened structures and tunnels for evacuation. Instead of being at the top of the building, the leadership would be underground, surrounded by specially built roofs and walls. The concept was simple and extraordinary at the same time.

"What do you think of it?" Gabriel sat across from Frank in Frank's office.

"I like the concept of the Alpha call signs. Do you think you can manage twenty-six teams?"

"We won't have twenty-six for quite some time. I have people out recruiting from the points of contact we have in the special forces world. There are several people who worked in major police agencies that I want to bring in. The FBI and Guardian have started working together. Hell, even the CIA wants us to assume some of their operations overseas."

Frank grunted the way his mom grunted when she didn't want to cross her dad but wanted to speak up.

"What?" Gabriel lifted an eyebrow and stared at him.

"Seems to me you have a logistics branch, a military operations element, which I'll come back to, an HR division, and support staff. You're missing training and vetting."

Gabriel nodded as he stared at the paper in front

of them. "Training. The men coming out of spec ops will be trained."

"But not as a team," Frank pointed out. "That, plus everyone needs to go through formal vetting. You only want the best. Those spec ops guys that get out may not have the cleanest record. The military is a microcosm of society. Bad apples in every walk of life. You don't want to have one of those rotten apples on your cart. That integrity, reputation, and morality you preach will take a hit the second one person screws up."

Gabriel picked up his pen and started writing. "I didn't think of that. My background is CIA. It makes sense to vet everyone." Gabriel kept writing. "Mental evaluations, too." Frank grunted in agreement.

Gabriel finished writing and looked up. "You were going to go back to the military operations element."

"Craig." Frank stared straight at his boss and friend.

"He's an acquired taste."

"He's an asshole. I'd keep him close. Put him under your thumb, Gabriel. He's one match shy of TNT status."

Gabriel put the pen down and rubbed his face. "He's been with me for a long time. I know he has issues." His friend leaned back in his chair. "I can't leave him behind."

"Don't. Not necessary, but you keep him in eyesight. He'll go off the rails if you don't."

Gabriel nodded. "Okay. Yeah, I get that. He's my responsibility." Gabriel sighed. "Where are you going to work now that we have this mapped out?" Frank grunted again, and Gabriel laughed. "What?"

"You don't have an intelligence section here. A place to gather information to route intel to your teams. You'll need to build one."

"Crap. I didn't give that to you, did I?" Gabriel picked up his briefcase and shuffled through the folders. "Here." He handed Frank a thick folder labeled "CCS."

Frank opened it and read through the proposal. "Compartmentalized Computer Section."

"Yes. They'd manage all information from all sections but not be part of the operations aspect. Compartmentalized to allow them to focus on information, not tactics, not operations, not what is happening or what will happen, just the scraping of information and the output when needed."

Frank nodded. "Good. What about communications?"

"I'm working on that. An operator system. We

have several candidates. Not military, so I see the need for that vetting." Gabriel pulled out another folder and showed Frank. "So, no holds barred, I need an honest opinion. Am I heading in the right direction? Does this structure seem viable to you?"

Frank leaned back. "You're heading in the right direction as far as I can tell, but I'm just a hick from South Dakota."

Gabriel snorted. "I've been doing my homework, Frank. You're a freaking genius. I have copies of the tests to prove it."

Frank grunted again. "Tests can't measure what you're looking for."

"But they can tell me when I'm on the right track. Stay here in D.C. and help me build this organization."

Frank shook his head. "I'll stay for the next year, but after that, I'll be back home. I think I can help the most with the hiring and vetting process. I know what to look for in military records. Warning flags I can see that maybe someone else couldn't. I can talk to commanders and teammates one on one."

Gabriel reached across the desk. "You're hired."

Frank snorted. "You already done hired me."

Gabriel laughed. "For the job as my VP in charge of my new Manpower Acquisition section."

Frank took the man's hand. "Anyone ever tell you that you like to get your way?"

Gabriel stood and grabbed his briefcase. "All the time. I'm heading over to my office. I'll gather the folders of men we were considering and bring them back."

"Hey, Gabriel," he called to his boss as he approached the door.

"Yo," the man said, turning back to face him.

"You're going to need a secretary. One who can herd cats." Frank leaned back and smiled. "One who won't be afraid to tell you off."

Gabriel nodded once. "Perfect. Find her for me." He opened the door and walked out.

Frank shook his head. "Shoved your boot in that one, didn't you, Marshall?"

# 9

*Present Day, Marshall Ranch, South Dakota:*

FRANK KEPT his attention on Tori while he talked about the CIA. He could see her surprise when he admitted he'd joined. He could see the emotions flash across her eyes. The shock, the disbelief, then the anger. She was mad he didn't tell her. Maybe hurt. He wasn't going to spray salt on the wound, but she'd asked for the complete truth, and that ball was rolling now.

"The CIA?" She looked at him. Her anger wasn't hidden.

"Why? What's wrong with Dad being in the CIA? He wasn't there long." Keelee stood up and headed to the bar to refill her wine glass.

"You could have told me." Tori ignored Keelee and continued to stare at her father.

Frank shrugged. "When you joined? I could have, but you needed to find your own way. I'd hoped the agency had changed by then."

Keelee stopped pouring her wine. "Excuse me? You were agency, Tori?"

Tori flicked her gaze over to Keelee. "You knew. You figured it out when I brought Jacob and the team home that first time."

"I figured out you were working in something other than computer security. No one has ever confirmed you worked for the CIA. Not to me."

Jacob leaned forward. "Hey, Keelee, Tori used to work for the CIA."

Keelee flipped Jacob off, and everyone laughed. Frank knew he wasn't off the hook with his younger daughter, but he'd deal with that issue later.

"You set up the initial hiring process for Guardian?"

Frank nodded. "And I found Daisy."

Anna smiled. "I loved her. He's never had a better secretary."

Gabriel nodded. "She was an amazing person, and she ran circles around me."

"She was a friend of Elizabeth's who was getting out of the military. She was an administrative specialist, and her ratings were top-notch. Plus, she had a secret clearance. Getting it upgraded was easier than initiating a new background check on a civilian." Frank nodded. "I wasn't above using my connections. Several of the secretaries who started with the organization came from the military. It was a hard life for women in the service back then."

"Still is." Ronan stood up and moved over to the food. "Sexual harassment is still a thing. Harder to spot but still in the culture, which sucks."

"It is all over, not just in the military," Jade added. "Not that anyone would try that with me."

"It is even out here in the Midwest. I've gone south to buy heavy equipment and had men suggest my husband come back to make the purchase." Keelee shook her head in dismay.

Adam laughed. "Like I'd know what to buy."

"That's my point. Just because I'm a woman doesn't mean I'm not able to run a ranch or purchase heavy equipment. It's not right."

"We do what we can to stop that type of thing."

Gabriel sighed. "It doesn't happen in any of my organizations."

"That you know of," Gabrielle said.

Gabriel nodded. "Point."

"So, how long did you stay in D.C.?" Keelee asked as she returned to her seat.

Frank adjusted his arm, pulling Amanda a bit closer.

*1980, Washington D.C.:*

FRANK'S OFFICE PHONE RANG, and he grabbed it, answering it while he scanned the folder in front of him. "Yes?"

"Frank?"

His head popped up, and he did a double-take at the phone. It took a second to pull himself out of his work and place the voice since she'd never called him at the office before. "Elizabeth?"

"Yeah, hey, could you come over tonight? I'd like to talk to you."

"Ah, well, yeah, I can. I'm sorry I haven't been around much. We've been so damn busy."

"No, that's okay. I just need to talk. You don't have to stay long."

He sighed and dropped back into his chair, looking at the mountain of folders on his desk. "You know what? I've become a file folder. Would you like to go out to dinner tonight?"

She didn't speak for a moment. "Maybe we could have something here?"

"That would be nice. I've been living on microwave dinners."

"God." Elizabeth made a retching noise.

"They aren't that bad."

She cleared her throat. "Yeah, they really are. I'll leave word at the desk downstairs. They'll let you up. About six?"

"I'll be there." He glanced at the clock. It was only four. He could get some more work done before he headed over.

"Good. I'll talk to you then."

Elizabeth hung up the phone, and his world reduced in size to the folder in front of him. Thank God he had the foresight to ask his secretary to let him know when it was twenty minutes to six. He would have worked right through their dinner. There was a sense of urgency in staffing and building Guardian, and everyone had succumbed to

Gabriel's dream. Someday the fledgling organization would be the epitome of the security world.

Once he was finished working, Frank walked over to her building. Getting a car at that time of night would be impossible, and he wasn't joking; he'd become a file folder. It had been forever since he'd stretched his legs. He missed the physical activity and being outdoors. Mostly, he missed open spaces. The view that Elizabeth had wanted was what he wanted, too. At night, when he was winding down from work, he'd taken to drawing up a house he'd build on the ranch. His pop and ma had given him a plot of land on the other side of the small valley from where they lived in the old house. He had grand dreams. He'd make it happen by harvesting trees from Marshall land. He could strip the pine bark and let them dry. He wanted a big dining room where his entire family would be able to sit at one table. A fireplace that would warm the coldest of nights and rooms that were spacious. Two wings, two stories, and a grand entrance. He smiled to himself as he waited to cross the street. One day, he'd have a porch swing and sit on it with his wife and take in the land and the beauty of South Dakota. At least, that was the dream.

He entered her building and went to the desk. "Frank Marshall."

"Yes, sir. This way." The man in a suit behind the desk went to the elevator, held the door open with his hand, inserted the key, hit the top floor, and stepped out, leaving Frank in the lift by himself. He tugged at his shirt cuffs, bringing them back down his arms and to the end of his suit jacket. The door opened, and he once again fixated on the view. Yes, he'd have an expansive view from his front porch. It was good to appreciate what you had. Here it was a view of the historic buildings. At home, it was a view of the splendor of nature. He'd take nature any day.

"Hi." At Elizabeth's greeting, he turned. She was pale and looked shaken. Something was wrong, terribly wrong. He could feel the wave of emotion radiate off her from where he stood.

"What happened?" He hustled across the room and was by her side in an instant.

She laughed, but it turned into tears. "I'm so sorry."

"Why, what happened?" He led her to the couch and pushed her golden hair away from her face. "What's wrong?"

"Frank, I'm pregnant." She lifted her blue eyes up

to him. "I haven't been with anyone but you ... for a while now. The doctor says I'm two months along."

A sucker punch to the gut would have winded him less. He heard the words, but the meaning wasn't coming through. "Pregnant?" The condom. The condom that broke. He swallowed hard but made sure he kept eye contact with Elizabeth.

Her blue eyes filled with tears, and she nodded. "I don't know what to do. I can't stay in the Navy. They're discharging me."

He knew that. It was the policy. Pregnant women were discharged immediately. "Okay." He finally took a breath. He looked at her. She was a wonderful woman, and they got along well. "Marry me."

She sniffed and gave a small bitter laugh, "Frank, you don't mean that. I don't want to trap you."

He squared his shoulders. "I do. I mean that. I can give you and our family a home, a good home. We're not poor ranchers, Elizabeth. I'm well off, and that ranch will be mine someday. We'll go to South Dakota, leave this insanity, and start fresh."

"You don't love me, Frank." She dropped her head into her hands and cried.

Frank pulled her into him and stroked her hair while she let her emotions flow. When she quieted, he spoke clearly, "Elizabeth Frazier, marry me. I loved you enough to make a baby with you. That feeling will only grow. I will devote my life to making you happy."

She lifted her head and stared at him. The puffy eyelids and red nose couldn't hide her disbelief. "You're sure?"

"I am. Is there any reason to stay here in D.C.?"

"Richard," she said and shook her head. "Damn him."

"Who's Richard?"

She sighed. "Richard Berkley. The man who destroyed my dreams. But that's over."

"This Berkley, will he come looking for you?" Frank wanted to know what was coming down the pike.

She sniffed. "No, Frank. He dumped me because his parents made him choose between me and their money. He chose the money. There isn't a reason for me to stay in D.C. I'll marry you. I'll leave with you."

He dropped a kiss onto her lips. "We'll make our way together. I'm going to give you a good life. Give our baby a good life. The feeling between us will grow." He'd fight hell and high water to make sure that happened.

She smiled up at him. "You are a wonderful man, Frank."

He leaned down. "I'm just a man. I do love you, Elizabeth." As he kissed her, he wondered if the type of love he felt for her would be enough. His gut told him it wouldn't, but he'd try like hell to prove himself wrong.

∽

"Why?" Gabriel blinked at him as if the words he was saying weren't computing.

"She's pregnant. I'm putting in my notice. I'll get whoever you want up to speed before I go. She's being discharged from the Navy. That's not an overnight process." Frank turned from the window and sat in the chair across from his boss.

"You're sure?"

Frank grunted. "Of what? That she's pregnant? Yes. That I'm going to marry her? Yes. That we're moving back to South Dakota? Yes. That I can get my replacement up to speed? Not really, depends on who you pick, but I'll give it a try."

Gabriel's eyes narrowed. "How long have you known her? Is she aware that you're rich?"

"I'm not rich," Frank grunted. Most of the wealth he had was left to him by his gramps. It was sizable, nothing like what his father had amassed. "I've known her for almost two years now. Met her when I came back from that first mission with you in Libya. We met by chance again here in D.C. There was nothing nefarious."

"'Nefarious'. Damn, what you hide behind that country demeanor." Gabriel slouched in his chair and ran his hand through his hair. "Okay, first, congratulations. Second, I'm not letting you off the hook. If you want to come back at any time, you call my number. I'll have you back in a heartbeat. I want you part of this organization. Buy in. Buy a percentage. I'm not offering it to anyone else, just you." Gabriel leaned forward and steepled his fingers.

"Why?"

"Because *you* believe in what I'm doing. You've never questioned my goals. Never told me I was a fool. You've supported me when those closest to me questioned and snipped at me. And because I believe you're going to come back. Eventually. Guardian *will* be a success. If nothing else, it's a smart hedge against the future. Don't look a gift horse in the mouth, Frank. That's a saying you country boys know, right?"

Frank grunted. "I have some money."

"I know." A shit-eating grin spread across Gabriel's face. "I've done my homework on those who work for me. Some backward hayseed told me I should do that. He has some smart moments."

Frank laughed and shook his head. "Did that hayseed tell you he'd kick your ass if you called him that again?"

Gabriel made a point to look like he was thinking. "No, can't say he did, but it might be good advice."

"It is." Frank sobered quickly. "I'll buy in, but I won't be back." He knew he was heading home for good. "I'm not cut out for this life. My heart is back in South Dakota. I was leaving in five months anyway."

"I would have done something to make you stay." Gabriel sighed.

"You would have tried," Frank acknowledged.

"You'll keep me posted on when you're leaving?"

"I will. Send me the paperwork for the percentage. I'll get it taken care of." He wasn't going to slide out the back door in the middle of the night. There'd be time.

"I don't want to lose you." Gabriel stood up and extended his hand.

Frank clasped it and smiled at his boss. "You were always going to."

. . .

*Present Day, Marshall Ranch, South Dakota:*

"He did sneak out on me." Gabriel winked at him.

Frank laughed. "Not true. You went overseas on a mission. Elizabeth's discharge went through. You knew it could happen."

Gabriel nodded. "I still say you snuck out."

"Wait, I thought you owned all of Guardian," Deacon shot toward his dad.

"Ninety percent. Frank Marshall owns ten percent."

"The income I used to expand and upgrade over the years. Well, some of it. Most is in the bank growing for the kids and grandkids." Frank took another sip of his whiskey.

"What did Grandma and Grandpa think of Mom when you brought her home?" Keelee was tucked up next to Adam.

Frank cocked his head and took another sip of whiskey before he answered that one. "Your mom wasn't cut from ranching cloth." Frank chuckled. "If it shed, got dirty, or tracked, she didn't want anything to do with it."

Joy grunted. "Your mom would have hated

Sasha. That poof has the entire house covered in white fur."

"Elizabeth was raised a city girl. She didn't cotton to most animals, and she didn't know the ranching life except what she'd seen on television, and that was the old westerns. Your mom was a neat freak, to be sure. She didn't like to get dirty much." *At all.* The woman was fastidious and hated any dirt inside the house. His mom was a good housekeeper, but at the end of the day, men and women covered in dirt had to get in and shower. Elizabeth would make a show of cleaning up anything tracked in, which didn't sit well with his mom, especially since that was the only time Elizabeth would pitch in.

"I bet that didn't go over well." Taty stood and went to the bar with her and Mike's glasses.

Frank grunted. The tension between his mom and Elizabeth was thick. Elizabeth didn't cook and didn't want to learn, so she mostly sat in the living room and watched television until she had Keelee. The arrival of her first granddaughter softened his mom a bit. Frank shrugged. "There was tension. But once we moved into this house, things quieted down." He'd moved them as soon as the kitchen and one bedroom were done. It calmed Elizabeth and helped keep the peace. Elizabeth even tried her hand at cooking. It was horrible, but he ate it. Eventually, there were four or five things she could make. He was appreciative of her trying.

"Did you love her?" Tori asked.

He nodded. "We grew in love together. Or, at least, I thought we had. We were close like married people are." He couldn't say they had an active sex life, but they did come together occasionally. "When she got pregnant with you, she was so happy. Because Keelee was just like me. She loved the animals on the ranch, hated wearing dresses and being coddled. Elizabeth prayed for a girl she could doll up. She thought Victoria would be the answer to everything she felt was missing. The loneliness and the feeling of being adrift. She told me that. That she felt out of step with everything on the ranch. I didn't know how much. I doubled down on teaching her about the ranch. She never took to the life, though she did love to ride."

"My father found her on one of those rides and killed her." Christian's words cut through the room like a razor-sharp knife.

Frank leaned forward, angry as hell. "You are not to blame for your old man's actions. Don't take that guilt on. I wouldn't allow it when we found out; I won't allow it now. You hear?"

Christian lifted his eyes to Frank. "Yes, sir." Jared pulled him back into his chest and whispered something into his ear. Christian nodded, and they kissed. He hated that Christian still thought he was somehow responsible for his father being a murderous reprobate.

Amanda's hand on his arm brought Frank back into his chair. "Sorry. Just gets me riled."

Christian smiled. "I understand."

"We all do," Amanda agreed. "I think we can skip that part of the story."

Anna agreed. "Absolutely. We know the circumstances and then about the letters you found much later."

"Oh, no. Hell, no. We aren't going to go one step further until they tell us about them meeting each other and falling in love." Jade pointed between her mom and Frank. "All we got was, 'Surprise, we're married.' *That* gap needs to be filled."

Every person in the room agreed with her except Gabriel and Anna. Tori whistled again, and everyone stopped. All eyes went toward the stairs. Talon appeared a few seconds later, asking, "What? We're being quiet, and the little ones are asleep. The movie is at the good part."

"Sorry, I'll come up if I need you. If you hear me whistle tonight, disregard," Tori said.

"Cool." Talon tapped the banister and headed back to the bunk room.

"I want to know why you weren't surprised when I asked to bring Jacob home first. I always wondered. You never flinched. Didn't ask any questions. Just said bring them home. That was out of the norm, especially after my situation in the CIA. You were so protective." Tori lifted an eyebrow at her father.

"You mean the accident that wasn't an accident." Keelee rolled her eyes. "I don't know any of you, do I?"

Adam wrapped his arms around her. "You know me, babe. That's all that matters." He kissed her on the forehead, and Keelee's bluster deflated.

Jacob leaned forward. "Hey, Keelee, my name's Jacob King, and I work for Guardian Security."

Keelee's jaw dropped open, and she lifted her hands upward. "Why?" Everyone laughed again.

Frank shook his head. Jacob never missed an opportunity to stir the pot or relieve the tension. Frank waited until the kids settled a bit.

Chad got up to get a soda. "Please don't let me stop you." He waved at Frank.

Frank finished his drink and handed it to

Gabriel. "We're both going to need one to get through the next part."

Gabriel took his glass and stood up. "Not sure I want to be involved," the man grumbled.

Frank snickered. "But you were. Up to your eyeballs."

"With what?" Tori asked. She was digging for the truth tonight, and by God, she'd get it.

"After this, I want to know about you and Mom," Jade chimed in again.

Frank rolled his eyes at the wild one. "Settle for a bit. I'll get to it." As impatient as a wild pony, that one.

Jade smiled widely. "Cool. I'll wait. Go ahead." She waved at him and got off Nic's lap, heading back to the bar.

"Tori graduated college and went to work for the CIA."

"I never told you that." Tori cocked her head.

Frank took the drink that Gabriel offered him. "Know that. I had Gabriel check in on you from time to time when you were at school."

Tori's mouth went slack and hung open. "I called you every week."

Frank nodded. "Know that. I answered the calls."

"Then why?"

"Because the world is an ugly place, Tori, and I could do it, so I did. No other reason than I wanted to take care of you." He shrugged. "I won't apologize for it. I'd do it again."

Tori shook her head. "What else don't I know?"

SEVENTEEN YEARS AGO, *Marshall Ranch, South Dakota:*

FRANK GLANCED at the calendar again. Almost seventy days without any word. That wasn't like Tori. Not at all. He glanced at the clock, then picked up the receiver and dialed the number he'd pulled out of the safe. It rang twice.

"Frank, you call to tell me you're coming back to work for me?" Gabriel's jovial tone stung a bit. He wished he was in a better mood to call, but hell, he needed more than a favor. "Frank? What's up? Are you reaching for a piece of that taffy?" Gabriel queried again.

"I need help." He forced the words out. It was against his nature to ask for help. Gabriel's casual check-ins on Tori aside, Frank had never extended a hand or felt so lost.

"What do you need? Say it, and you've got it."

"Tori. She's been out of contact for seventy days. I think she was on an op. Said it could be a couple weeks before she called."

"The agency hasn't contacted you?" Gabriel quizzed.

"No."

"Then she's still alive, or they've lost her and are covering it up. What do you know about her position, what she does?"

"Not much, just what I've gotten from inference." He gave Gabriel what he had.

"I'm owed big time by the CIA. I'll get what I can. If she's out there, I'll find her and bring her back to you."

"Thank you." His skin prickled as a wave of relief washed over him.

Gabriel hesitated for several seconds before he spoke again, "She might not be alive, Frank."

His eyes snapped shut, and he ground out the words, "I know."

"I'll pull every string I can. I need her date of birth, social security number, and a recent photo. Do you have a fax machine?"

"I do. I'll send the latest picture I have." He rattled off Tori's birthday. "I'll get her social. It's on my tax documents."

"Never mind. I'll have my CCS people pull it off that."

"They can do that?" Frank asked.

"You filed electronically?"

"I did back when it first started up." He didn't any longer. Didn't trust his information floating out there.

"Then they can do that. Will you be coming to D.C.?"

"Not planning on leaving the ranch unless there's a reason to travel." Frank could hear the tapping of a keyboard as they talked.

Gabriel spoke when the typing ceased. "I just sent an action item to my CCS. They'll start by scanning facial recognition at airports; it's new technology. Disregard the picture. I forgot they could access the passport archives. I'll get what information I can and work it hard and fast."

Frank blinked at the absurd speed and ability of the computer section. That's why he hated any type of electronic device. It left a trail. "Thank you."

"Frank, I'll find her. Bank on that."

"I am," he said before hanging up. If she wasn't alive, he might have to go back to D.C., but he'd be going with a purpose and intent. It wouldn't be pretty for anyone.

Two long weeks later, he received a call at two in the morning. He grabbed at the phone and answered, "Tori?"

"No, it's Gabriel. I think we found where she is, or at least, we've narrowed her location down. I have a team inside the country now, close to where she might be. I'm heading to Germany. Once I recover the team, I'll go with them back into Afghanistan, and we'll find her."

"Afghanistan?" He rubbed his face. "What the fuck is she doing over there?"

"Long story, and I'll brief you later. I have to leave now. I'll call you as soon as I know anything." Gabriel disconnected the line.

Frank put the receiver back into the cradle, then clasped his hands together. "God, please protect her. Please let Gabriel find her alive."

*Present Day, Marshall Ranch, South Dakota:*

"That's why you were in Germany when we made it back to Ramstein." Jacob cocked his head. "You were pissed we brought her out of country."

Gabriel shook his head. "No, I was pissed I didn't

know about it sooner. Protocol would have been to call in that you were bringing out an American. I should have fired you."

"Again," everyone in the room said at the same time.

Jacob lifted his arms. "I haven't been fired since I married Tori. Well, maybe once or twice, but seriously, I've done better."

"I think he protests too much." Jillian giggled and turned to Drake. "You're going to have to fill me in on the background of *that* story."

Drake smiled and winked at his wife. "Skipper had a propensity to deviate from protocol."

"Thanks for the backup, asshole." Jacob flopped back onto the couch cushion.

"Anyway, when I got word that a female was on board and inbound in need of medical, I called Frank and got two sentences out before the CIA crawled up my ass and your bird landed."

"What did you tell him?" Tori asked.

"'She's alive. I'll call later.'" Frank provided the words that had sent him to his knees.

"How did the CIA know?"

"A question that I asked. I got stonewalled, so I went to the top, and they went down to the director of the CIA. Heads rolled. It was an unsanctioned op where Tori would be the diversion and give up false information. She didn't."

Tori's eyes misted, and she shook her head. "I trusted them."

"Heads rolled. By the time we got answers, Tori had been brought back to the States, and we were able to get her released." Gabriel nodded. "She was used by people who were seeking political and information leverage. She withstood ninety days of torture and didn't give up anything. Their operation failed because Tori was strong and Jacob arrived in time. Information is power to some people, and they didn't care how they got it."

"Oh, shit, Tori. I didn't know." Keelee reached over and grabbed her sister's hand. Tori nodded but didn't say anything.

Frank continued, "Gabriel called me back a couple hours later with the details he knew. I asked for the names of the men who had saved her. Gabriel faxed me your names and a brief bio on all of you. That's how I knew the team before you called and asked if you could bring Jacob home to heal."

Jacob leaned forward. "So, that day you were in the tack room listening to what was happening, you knew Tori was going to be with me."

"And probably working for Guardian. Yes." Frank nodded.

Jewell raised her hand. Frank chuckled. "Jewell, you have a question?"

"Ummm ... yeah, there's a problem with this sequence of events. *I* didn't know Frank worked for Guardian. I have all the records from the beginning of the business. I would have known."

"Because I shredded them before they could be digitized. Before I got married, it was in my will that Frank Marshall would take over operation of Guardian. He didn't know it, but I wouldn't leave my life's work in anyone else's hands."

Frank whipped his head in Gabriel's direction. "Hell-bent on getting me off the ranch, weren't you?"

Gabriel chuckled. "Maybe."

**10**
---

A cry on one of the baby monitors disrupted the gathering, and Frank was grateful for it. Tori had handled the info dump pretty well, but he still wanted to talk with her alone.

"That one is mine." Joy jumped up from the couch. "Go ahead. I'll get the lowdown later."

Faith stood up. "I'm going to get the boys into bed, and I know Rachel will be waking up hungry soon."

"We should put Marcus to bed," Christian said, standing up.

Frank stood up and looked directly at Tori. "We can finish up the stories tomorrow night."

Jasmine stood and pulled Chad up. "Let's go up

and get the kids. We'll be in California tomorrow night, but I'll get the lowdown from Jewell or Jade."

Most everyone moseyed out of the big room and went back to where they were staying for the night. Frank carried trays to the kitchen, helping Amanda and Anna before returning to the living room. Tori and Jacob were the only ones remaining.

"Joseph and Ember are getting our boys settled," Tori said as Frank sat down.

He nodded. "Good."

"Why didn't you tell me about any of this?" Tori leaned forward, her elbows resting on her knees as she stared at him.

He held her gaze. "What good would it have done? What difference would it have made? I told you I spent ten years away from the ranch. I was never dishonest. I told you I traveled, and I served in the Navy for a time, then worked a couple other jobs before I came back home to the ranch."

"Deceit by omission is still deceit," Tori whipped back at him.

Frank leaned forward and matched her position. Fair answer, but he'd made that call based on the fact that he'd done things that had nothing to do with the ranch and what his family knew about him. He'd do it again, and he wouldn't be taken to task for something she'd do herself if she were in his position. "Ask yourself what you're mad at right now, little girl. Is it me you're angry with? Are you mad that I had a life you didn't know about? One that didn't involve you? Are you mad at things you couldn't control and didn't have any input into because you hadn't been born yet? Or are you mad I kept tabs on you and I was going to find you when the Agency was willing to let you be a pawn in an unsanctioned op? Why are you angry, Tori?"

Jacob ran a hand up her back and gripped her neck gently. Tori's eyes closed, and she shook her head. "Since Jacob rescued me from that damn camp, my life has been a lie."

Jacob stilled. "What?" he asked quietly.

"Did you know my dad had asked Gabriel for help?"

Jacob shook his head. "I didn't know a damn thing. Nothing that transpired between the two of us was contrived by anyone. What lie are you talking about?"

Tori stood up and ran her fingers through her hair. "I don't know. God, I just don't know. I just feel that if I'd known this, all of this, the event with Richard wouldn't have happened. He wouldn't have taken Faith and me; he wouldn't have tried to kill us. Amari wouldn't have fucked with my brain."

Jacob stood up and wrapped his wife in his arms. "None of us were responsible for Richard Berkley's actions except for Richard Berkley. He was the only one responsible for the horror that happened. I failed you. I should have killed Amari when I had the chance. If you want to blame someone, blame me for not putting him out of humanity's misery. The slimy son of a bitch."

Tori dropped against her husband. "I'm sorry." She turned so she was talking to him. "Daddy, I'm so messed up. I'm not mad at you. I'm just so ... lost."

Frank swallowed hard and stood up. She moved from Jacob's arms to his. He held her against him and hushed her cries like he had when she was little. "You have Jacob, and you have me. You'll find your way out of the darkness. We're here with you. You aren't alone."

She nodded and sniffed. "I know." She stepped back and wiped her eyes. "I'll call Jeremiah and ask if I can see him in the morning." She moved next to Jacob. "I want to hear how you and Amanda fell in love." She smiled, but it was half-hearted.

"So do I." Jacob put his arm around Tori's shoulders. "But we'll leave that for tomorrow night."

# 11

Amanda glanced at the trays and pulled an extra one out for the bunkroom. "Anna, would you grab one of those big plastic bowls out of that cupboard?" She pointed to the one in question.

"Got it. Chips or those cracker fish things?" Anna asked as she walked across the kitchen.

Amanda stopped mixing dip. "Better get two bowls and put out both. Those boys can consume their weight in snacks."

"Even after a huge meal," Anna agreed. "Ronan and Deacon ate us out of house and home several times."

"You should have had five hanging around. Goodness, there were days I didn't think I could stretch the budget far enough." Amanda shook her head. "But we managed. Thanks to Gabriel."

"The man should have a halo," Anna sniggered. "He's put up with me and the kids' shenanigans. He's up for sainthood, let me tell you."

"I know Charley caused a little bit of a tither when she went to work for Guardian. What has Gabrielle done?"

"Nothing. Mom, don't spread rumors. I'm an angel." Gabrielle walked in and grabbed one of the filled trays. "Bunkroom?"

"Yes, please." Amanda held open the swinging door, and Gabrielle stepped out as quickly as she'd entered.

"Gabby is the caretaker of the family. She herds her brothers and Charley, but she isn't an angel." Anna leaned in and whispered, "She takes after her mom."

Amanda laughed. "I don't think that's a bad thing." They finished building another tray for the bunkroom. "I'll take these up and meet you in the living room. These evening chats have become addictive. Almost like a soap opera but with real people."

Amanda snorted. "I'm one of the real people in that soap tonight."

Anna stopped. "You know, no one would blame you if you didn't want to talk about your courtship with Frank."

Amanda turned around and pushed a strand of hair that had escaped her ponytail back over her ear. "I don't mind. Frank is intensely private, so we'll skip over the sexy parts." At least in their talk. She would remember every minute of her time with her husband.

"I'm sure the children will appreciate that. They don't think parents can have sex." Anna made a face.

"Little do they know." Amanda waved her hand at the door, and Anna's laughter followed her out into the hall.

She grabbed the handles of the tray filled with small bowls of snacks and backed out of the kitchen. Frank stopped as she opened the door, almost colliding with her.

"Let me get this for you. Is there anything else?" He looked past her to the kitchen as he took the tray.

"No. This is the last of it."

They walked down the hall together, but Frank stopped before they turned the corner into the living room. "Our story is something I don't fancy telling." It was personal, and the way he was raised, you kept personal things private.

She put her hand on his arm, still strong with muscle. "Frank, if we tell them our love story, then they can tell their children or grandchildren. When we're long gone, our story, our love for each other, will still be remembered."

He blinked and then smiled. "You're not getting rid of me for many, many years."

Amanda toed up and kissed her husband. "I love you, too."

She followed him into the living room and sat down while Frank got them both a drink. They usually had coffee on the porch after dinner, but when the children came home, they would have cocktails. She accepted the whiskey sour he made for her and held both of their glasses as he got comfortable beside her. The crowd had thinned tonight. Jasmine and Chad had left for California. Joy and Dixon were staying at their home to try to keep Kai on some semblance of a schedule, which was one thing Faith didn't have to worry about. Rachel could and would sleep through a tornado, which helped since her brothers could be as loud as one sometimes.

Jade, however, was front and center with a bag of popcorn in her lap. Jewell walked into the room and dropped three bags of chocolate on the table. Jacob grabbed one, poured half out on his lap, twisted the bag, and launched the rest of it to Jason.

The man snatched it out of the air and winced. "Little more notice next time, bro," Jason growled at Jacob but settled back with the candy. Christian took another bag, and he, Jared, and Jewell divided up the spoils.

Gabriel and Anna took their usual seats, and Keelee and Adam were in the oversized chair that Jade and Nic occupied the night before. Mike, Taty, Drake, and Jillian had the floor today. She smiled at her family. If not by blood, then by love. Their lives were interwoven into a singular fabric. One that was stronger because of the combination.

"So ..." Jade held up her hands. "Spill."

Amanda lifted an eyebrow at her daughter. "Excuse me, darling, who put you in charge?"

"Mom, one, nobody, but that has never mattered, and two, I want to know. We could have finished this last night."

"No. That was my fault." Tori shook her head. "It took a long time to digest what was said. I don't think I would have listened to anything past where we left off last night." She glanced over at Jade. "My issues, not yours. Sorry."

Jade's shoulders dropped. "Aww ... shit. I didn't

mean anything by that, Tori. We all know you got screwed. You and Faith got fu .... ah, sucker-punched."

Faith snorted and waved at her face. "Punched is right. I have perfect teeth now." She smiled widely, showing off her new teeth. "Silver linings." Faith leaned back against Jason, who wrapped a big arm around her shoulders.

"So, Mom, how did you and Frank become a thing?" Jewell asked before she popped a chocolate into her mouth. Zane reached over and took all but three from her lap. Jewell frowned at him but shrugged, taking control of the three pieces he'd left her.

"We met at the hospital in virgina." Frank looked at her.

She smiled. "I was kept in the dark for quite some time that my boys were in harm's way." Amanda leaned forward and stared at Gabriel.

The man groaned. "I promised. Never again."

Anna grunted, imitating Frank's "I'm calling that bullshit" grunt. The laughter made her heart lighter. "Anyway, Justin met me at the airport and spilled the beans."

"Justin usually is tighter-lipped on most things." Gabriel sighed. "She called as soon as things settled at the hospital and chewed my ear off."

Anna reached up and touched his ear. "Still there."

Gabriel rolled his eyes.

"Wait, what needed settling at the hospital?" Jade reached into the popcorn bag again. Her eyes were wide, and she motioned with her empty hand for them to continue.

SEVENTEEN YEARS AGO, *Undisclosed hospital in Virginia:*

AMANDA FOLLOWED her son Justin down the hospital corridor. The air was tinged with the antiseptic smell of strong cleaners. "Jason and the others are in a private wing." He turned the corner and waited for her to catch up.

"Sorry." She hustled a bit.

"Don't be. Remember, the doctors said it was only a matter of time before he wakes up."

Amanda nodded. She'd been clinging to those words. She wasn't about to forget them. "The other men?"

"Dixon and Drake from Jacob's team. You've met them, right?"

"I have." The twins were amazing young men.

"There are a couple others from the team Jason was leading, but they'll be discharged soon. Fractures, some wounds from the conflict they were caught up in." Justin didn't go into what type of conflict they were involved in, and she didn't ask.

"Jacob's wife, Victoria, right?" She'd been shocked that Jacob had gotten married. Even more shocked that she hadn't been told, but it was her son's life.

"Yeah. She goes by Tori. She's here with the twins. Her father is usually here, too. They're good people, Mom. They make sure everyone is getting the care they should."

Justin pushed the button on the outside of the doors. A voice sounded through the speaker. "May I help you?"

"Justin King with my mother."

"Stand by, sir. There has been a bit of a disturbance."

Amanda's heart thundered in her chest. "A disturbance?" She looked up at her son.

His eyes widened. "I don't have a clue."

Five minutes later, the door opened, and an

armed guard let them in. Amanda gaped at the man who passed her, his arm clearly broken under the skin. "What happened to him?"

"I think I know." Justin quickened his pace and made it to the doorway before she did. What she saw was disturbing. "Oh, Mary, Joseph, and the three wise men." She whispered her words, too shocked to say them any louder.

The room was a disaster, and her son lay strapped to the bed. She'd bet anything her son Jason had broken that man's arm.

Justin's voice brought all attention to the doorway. "I think I may have just the person."

Amanda stepped into the room, her eyes steadfast on her son. Good lord, what had happened? She moved to the bedside. Her sweet child. He'd been through so much. *Too* much. There was an IV bag on the ground, and Jason's bandaged arm told the story as plain as daylight. Amanda cupped her son's face in her hands and kissed his forehead. She shook her head and then searched for the medical authorities in the room. Aggravation at a multitude of scenarios floated to the surface of her normally calm demeanor. She looked at the doctor and delivered a lecture that even the most obstinate two-year-old would understand. "My son is a recovering drug addict. He fought hard to get off prescription drugs and has been clean for years now. He apparently saw the IVs and reacted accordingly. When you wake him up, you make sure he has nothing attached to him. If you've been giving him narcotics, write a list of what you've given him and when. He needs to be in control of his care. It's the only way he can cope." She didn't want to lose her control and yell at the man, so she squared her shoulders and turned to the others in the room. An absolutely beautiful tall blonde stood beside a broad-shouldered man. The woman could only be one person—she hoped. She smiled and greeted her new daughter-in-law with a kiss on the cheek. "Victoria, I'm so sorry we met like this. Welcome to the family. I'm Amanda King, the 'mother.'"

Tori smiled and squeezed her hand. The girl's smile was genuine and loving. *Oh, what a relief. Jacob's chosen wisely, hasn't he?*

Tori turned to the man beside her. He was tall and strongly built, and Amanda would guess he was in his fifties. *My, does he make his fifties look good.* She felt her eyes widen as she internalized what she'd thought. *Goodness, inappropriate much, Amanda?*

"Mrs. King, this is my father, Frank Marshall."

Frank nodded, barely managing a choked, "Ma'am."

She smiled at the blush that rushed to his cheeks. Goodness, it had been forever since she'd had an effect on a man. She extended her hand and touched his arm. "My name is Amanda, not Mrs. King or ma'am. Frank, it was good of you to come out for your daughter."

Frank cleared his throat and nodded. Amanda held his gaze. Finally, he broke their connection. "Came for her and my boys. Done adopted Jacob and his team. Dixon and Drake both are laid up. Taking them back home with me as soon as they can travel."

Frank returned the chair that had been tossed to the side of the room back to Jason's bed and motioned to it.

*A gentleman, too.* Goodness, if she'd met him in any other way, she would have embarrassed herself, but he wasn't the reason she was there, and she needed to deal with the issues at hand before dreaming of Prince Charming. Especially at her age. She shook her head. "Oh, thank you, no. I've been sitting all day. Justin, honey, would you take my bags to the Georgetown house before you go to the restaurant?"

"Yes, ma'am. Jewell knows you're here. I just sent a text. She'll be back shortly. If you need anything, just give me a call. I can be back in no time."

She sighed and shook her head. "Darlin', I'll be okay. I know you've been staying here most nights with Mr. Marshall. Go take care of your business and maybe get some sleep? Bless you. You look so tired." She cupped his face and lifted up on her toes, kissing him on the cheek.

"Yes, ma'am. I'll try." Justin pulled her into a huge bear hug. "Love you, Momma."

"Love you, too, baby." She watched him walk down the hall and took a deep breath before she turned to Victoria.

"All right, daughter-in-law, let me have it." Amanda pegged her new daughter-in-law with a stare.

Jacob's wife snapped her head up and blinked repeatedly. "Excuse me? Have what?" The girl was confused, so she helped her out.

"Where are my sons? Why are they not here? I know where Jasmine and Jade are and what they're doing. Jewell, Jason, and Justin are accounted for. That leaves my core troublemakers. Where are they?"

Victoria closed her eyes. "I don't know. They're

missing. We haven't heard from them, and we can't find them."

Dear God, that wasn't good. She needed her sons to come home. If they were in trouble, she prayed they had each other. She whispered, "Are they together?"

"Yes, ma'am. The last we heard, Joseph was meeting Jacob and Jared."

She jumped and grabbed Victoria's arm. "Joseph is with them?" When Tori nodded, she drew the first deep breath since she'd walked into this hospital. Okay. Things would be okay. She squared her shoulders and nodded. "Well, then, let's get these boys healing. When Joseph and the young ones have finished their work, they'll contact you."

Tori looked at her, baffled. She got it. No one knew about Joseph. Well, except for Gabriel. Her oldest was ... Well, he was who and what he was, and she loved him without reservation.

Tori shook her head and asked, "How can you be so sure, Amanda?"

How did she answer that truthfully? *By hedging the truth.* She smiled. "Because, honey, Joseph is probably the single most-driven force God has ever put on this planet. Combine him with Jacob and Jared, who are smart, resourceful, and damn good at what they do, and they become invincible. Now, would you quit questioning what I know to be a certainty and regale me with the love story that is Victoria and Jacob while we wait for Jason to wake up again?"

## 12

*Seventeen years ago, Undisclosed hospital in Virginia:*

FRANK SLOWLY EASED out of Jason's room and headed back to the boys. Dixon had woken up, which was good. The doctors assured Frank that the wounds would heal, but the injuries sucked him back to his time in the SEALs. Medical technology had come so far in the span of life between then and now. He pulled the chair from the wall, placed it between the beds, leaned back, and closed his eyes. As was now his custom, he thanked his maker for the boys making it back and asked for a helping hand getting the others home. It was a tempest of a situation, and he had no idea if they'd ever be found alive. Tori was worried sick and splitting time between trying to find them and holding vigil with his team. Maybe now that Amanda King had arrived, Tori would stop trying so hard to be everything to everyone.

He grunted to himself. *As if.* His daughter would burn both ends of the candle until she collapsed. Frank checked each of the boys' monitors. When he'd first arrived, he had no idea what all the bells and whistles were about. He cornered a nurse and had her explain the contraptions and what they did. He knew what normal range was now and when he should be concerned. They were holding their own today. That was why he'd wandered down to Jason's room.

Damn, that boy was strong. The orderly's arm snapped like a twig in Jason's grip. A mountain of a man who was frantic, scared, and lost. If only the medical people had slow-rolled the response when they saw he had it handled. But that was hindsight, and hindsight was only good in teaching lessons. Wishing for things to be different never got the different done.

That mom, though. Amanda. She was a force, just like her kin he'd met. They took after her in looks and personality. All of them. Frank crossed his boot over one knee and placed his cowboy hat on his opposite knee. She was something. Beautiful in a way not many women were. She didn't wear a lick of makeup that he could see. Her black hair was swept up into some kind of comb-clamp thingy, and damn, did she command attention. He'd be lying if he said he didn't notice her body. She was trim, and her bare arms were muscled. She was accustomed to hard work, or she worked out in one of those fancy gyms. He rolled his neck. Couldn't see that, though. Didn't strike him as a city girl or a gym-spa type. But he could be wrong on all points. Lord knows his track record with women was less than pristine.

There had been the occasional woman after Elizabeth died. He'd dated a time or two. Just didn't send sparks flying, and he wasn't going to settle. Not that he regretted his time with Elizabeth. God, far from it. His daughters were his world. It sucked knowing that his wife had died unhappy. He wasn't going to delude himself. She didn't fit. Round peg, triangle hole. That was why he was so damn adamant that the girls do what they loved. It was why he let Victoria live her life. But damn it, he hated it for her. Keelee, well, that girl would run the ranch someday. She never took out. Didn't want to go to college. Didn't want to leave the ranch for any length of time. She'd never traveled and never had the urge to do so. She was just like her grandma. Maybe he should have forced her to experience the world, but that wasn't his oldest. She was of the land. Marshall land.

"Mr. Marshall?"

Frank jerked around and damn near face-planted when he tried to stand up too quickly. Amanda King stood in the doorway. "Frank, ma'am. Please call me Frank."

Amanda smiled at him and walked into the room. "Jason is out of it. The doctors tell me it'll be some time before he wakes. I thought I'd come to check on the Wonder Twins." She nodded to his boys.

He chuckled. "They are a matched set of trouble; I'll give you that." He and the boys had clicked. They'd needed a father, and damn it, he'd stepped straight into that role without a second thought. Those boys were special.

"In a good way. I think a lot of their shenanigans are because they don't want anyone to look too close." Amanda put her hand on Drake's leg. "They never had anyone but themselves. You can tell."

Frank swallowed hard. "I could see it. I've told

them my home is theirs. They'll come home with me when they can travel."

Amanda nodded. "As Jason will with me. He fought off a bad, medically prescribed painkiller addiction. I watched him struggle minute by minute some days. I understand why he freaked out."

"He wasn't too with it. Could have some memory issues because of the injuries." Frank motioned to the chair. "Care to sit?"

Amanda smiled and sat on the chair. Frank leaned against the foot of Dixon's bed. "Sorry the kids didn't tell you about the nuptials."

She smiled briefly. "I raised independent children. Maybe too independent in some cases, but my approval or knowledge of their spouses isn't required. Victoria is a wonderful young lady, by the way. I was able to convince her to go home and rest."

Frank chuckled. "You've worked a miracle, then. I couldn't get her out of here with a crowbar."

"A mother has a way of suggesting things and making a child believe it was their own idea. It's a genetic thing. I'd tell you the secret, but you're not in the mom club." Amanda leaned forward. "Is that supposed to be that high?" She pointed to the oxygen reading.

"The higher, the better." Frank nodded.

"Oh, good." She dropped back into the chair. "I spent my fair share of time in hospitals with five boys and three girls who wouldn't be left behind and had to be involved with their brother's mischief. It has been a while, though. While much of this is the same, it's different, too."

Frank nodded. "Haven't been in a hospital since I got out of the Navy many moons ago."

Amanda turned to him. "Naval man? But don't you live in South Dakota?"

"Yes, ma'am, I do."

"What made you join the Navy?"

He shrugged. "My folks encouraged me to leave the ranch, to make sure it was the life I wanted. The Navy seemed like a way to see the world."

"And did you? See the world?"

Frank smiled down at her. The question could have been polite, a way to pass the time, but she seemed genuinely interested. "Yes, ma'am. One mission at a time."

Amanda's eyebrows rose, and she looked toward the door before she spoke, "Oh. So, you were spec ops."

Now that was a leap, wasn't it? "How would you know that?" He was genuinely curious. The woman was either a mind reader or ...

She glanced at the door and then leaned forward. "You know my children work for Guardian, right?"

Frank nodded. "I heard that from Jacob, yes."

"I listen, Frank. I might not approve of some of the risks they take, but I know what they do and why they do it." She held up a hand. "Nothing specific, just in general terms."

"I was a SEAL, then CIA for a bit before I worked for Guardian." And holy hell, that was more than he'd told anyone about his past.

"With Gabriel?" Amanda turned more toward him. He nodded. "He's been a lifesaver for the kids and me. My late husband started working with him as a second job in the eighties. When Chance was killed on the job, the life insurance policy that Gabriel's company had taken out for Chance gave us a way to survive. I worked when I could, but raising eight babies by yourself is hard work."

Frank grunted. "Couldn't imagine. I went crazy with worry about the two I have."

"Tori isn't your only child, then?"

"No, ma'am, I have an older girl. Keelee. She's as different from Tori as night is from day, but they could pass as twins."

Amanda cocked her head. "What am I going to have to do to get you to call me Amanda?"

"It'll come in time." He hoped. He'd like to get to know the woman better.

"Hi, Mr. Marshall. I'm going to change Drake's bandages now."

"And that is our cue to exit." He extended his hand to Amanda to help her stand. She placed her hand on Drake's foot and looked over at Dixon. "Keep healing, boys." She turned and walked out with him following her. "We can go down to Jason's room," she suggested.

Frank glanced at his watch. "They're serving dinner in the mess downstairs. Excuse me, cafeteria. Could I bring you something up? We can share a meal and visit in Jason's room while he sleeps. He'll need you there when he wakes up again."

"Oh, that would be heavenly. Thank you so much. I'm not a picky eater. Anything you're getting is fine with me." Amanda backed down the hall as she spoke. "I'm glad I met you, Frank." She smiled and turned, heading down the hall.

He did an about-face and headed out of their wing. After the guard shut the door behind him, a smile twitched at the corner of his lips. He was glad he'd met her, too.

. . .

*Present Day, Marshall Ranch, South Dakota:*

"Aww ... that's so sweet." Jade sighed.

Amanda glanced at her daughter and made a point to correct her wild one. "We had a lot in common."

Jade squeaked, "I wasn't being sarcastic, Mom. I meant it."

Frank chuckled. "We spent a lot of hours shuffling between hospital rooms. Once everyone was out of the woods, we got to know each other better."

Jason leaned forward. "I was really messed up when I woke up again, but I remember knowing that I trusted you, Frank, and that you were safety. I hadn't met you, but your face and confidence were crucial. I was glad my mom was with you when they brought me out of it the second time. I know that seems bogus, but it felt right that you were with her. Once my mind cleared, that feeling remained."

"He got through to you when you were thrashing around the first time you woke up. I think that was what your subconscious registered. That he was there to help you. I've never seen anyone snap an arm like that." Tori shook her head. "Like a twig."

Jason shifted on the couch. "Don't even recall

doing that."

Faith turned and smiled up at him. "You wouldn't have done it if you were yourself. You're nothing but a big ol' marshmallow."

Jacob snorted his drink, then coughed. Tori beat him on the back as he tried to breathe. When he could, he looked at Faith. "Not a marshmallow. You don't work for him."

Jewell cocked her head. "I do. He's a marshmallow."

Jade agreed. "Totally. A big, squishy center."

Jason rolled his eyes. "Enough with the marshmallow talk."

Taty joined in. "Did you know they have marshmallows with chocolate on the inside now?"

"Oh, my God, I so want some." Jewell turned to stare at Zane, who closed his eyes and dropped his head back. "Please, baby." Jewell snuggled up to him.

"You'll be climbing the walls. Sugar is not your friend, no matter what you think." Zane opened his eyes and looked at his wife.

"I used to live on sugar!"

"We know," Jacob, Joseph, and Jason said at the same time.

"Hey!" Jewell sat up and glared at her brothers.

"I didn't say a word." Jared held up his hands.

"That's why you're my favorite brother right now." Jewell crossed her arms and dropped back next to Zane.

"We should make s'mores," Jillian said suddenly.

Drake blinked at her and smiled. "Sounds great."

Jillian turned toward the couch where Amanda sat. "Amanda, do you have everything? We can make them and listen to your love story."

Amanda narrowed her eyes. "I think I do. Are we calling the kids down?"

Jacob shook his head. "Nope. They have enough junk food up there to last them." He stood and offered his hand to Tori. "Kitchen, bathroom, and bar break. Huddle up in ten."

Amanda looked over at Frank. "Were we just ordered around in our own house."

Frank watched as everyone scattered. "I do believe the inmates are running the asylum, yes."

# 13

*Present Day, Marshall Ranch, South Dakota:*

"So, Amanda, when did you know you were in love with Frank?" Jillian asked as she roasted four marshmallows on a skewer. Drake was busy snapping graham crackers and chocolate bars into matching squares.

Amanda glanced at her husband. "I knew he was special very early on."

Frank lifted her hand to his lips and kissed the back of it. "For me, too."

There was a collective sigh from the women, and

Amanda's heart filled with the love she had for her husband.

*Seventeen years ago, Jacob's Georgetown home in Virginia:*

Amanda glanced at herself in the mirror. She'd borrowed a navy blue dress from Jasmine. It was straight cut and hugged her hips and waist. The neckline was a bit too low for her, so she'd found a silk scarf and wrapped it around her neckline, draping it over one shoulder and securing it with a pin. She tucked her hair back behind her ears. It was the best she could do. She hadn't worn makeup since Chance had passed. There wasn't any need, nor did she have the desire, but right then, she wished she had some mascara and maybe some blush.

Jasmine had an entire cabinet filled with perfumes and lotions. She dabbed a floral one on her wrist and gave herself another once-over.

She smiled, then shook her head at herself. "You're acting like a schoolgirl." Grabbing her purse before walking out the door, Amanda squared her shoulders and drew a deep breath before heading downstairs.

Frank was waiting for her. She stood at the top of the stairs, and he hadn't seen her yet. His jeans were new and pressed, his western-yoked shirt similarly pressed. He carried his felt Stetson in his hands. She noticed his boots had been polished, too. So, she wasn't the only one who thought tonight was special.

He must have sensed her because he turned. A smile spread across his face, and he gave a low whistle. "You doll up nicely, Amanda."

She laughed and walked down the stairs. "Thank you. You look nice, too." She crossed the room to him. He cleared his throat and started to say something but stopped. "What is it?"

He turned his hat in his hands for a moment. "It's been two weeks since we met. The boys are on the mend. We probably won't be here much longer. Fact is Dixon and Drake's doctor is going to clear them to travel in the next couple of days."

She sighed and nodded. "Jason is doing wonderfully, and we'll be gone shortly, too."

Frank reached for her hand and brought it up, holding it between them. "I don't want to lose this friendship."

Amanda linked her fingers through his. She

glanced up at him. "Frank, I'm sorry. I don't think of this as a friendship."

She watched his face as it fell. The eagerness she'd seen earlier melted away. "Oh," he said and dropped her hand.

She reached for his arm. "I'd like to think of it as more, Frank. I want more than a friendship with you."

He blinked at her. The deer in the headlights look lasted longer than she expected. Finally, she stepped in, toed up, and kissed him on the lips. The kiss was all her for about two seconds, then his arm wrapped around her. Sweet Mary, Joseph, and the three wise men, he consumed her with that kiss. A shiver traveled through every nerve in her body, and electricity snapped between them.

When he lifted his head, she had to hang on to his shoulders she was so dizzy. "Wow." She opened her eyes.

"You can say that again." Frank dipped down and kissed her again. This time it was a searching, passionate kiss. A lifetime had passed since she'd last drawn a fantastic male scent into her lungs and tangled it with a need that left her breathless. She leaned against him and felt his desire. Parts of her that she'd thought had withered and died blossomed with those kisses. When he lifted his head again, she let herself savor the feeling before she opened her eyes. He was staring at her, and she could see the need burning in his eyes. "I want more than friendship with you, too." His words were hoarse, almost guttural.

Amanda smiled up at him and lifted her finger, tracing his lips. "I'm going to be up-front with you, Frank. It's been a long time for me. I'm not the type of person to let go of my reserve easily. I would like our children not to know about us until we know what's happening."

He still held her against him as a smile spread across his face. "I think we understand each other. My children have no say in my private life. I'm a man of singular determination, Amanda. That means it's just you and me."

She leaned back and lifted an eyebrow. "Just what type of a lady do you think I am, Frank Marshall?"

He jerked her back against him. "Mine," he growled right before he kissed her again. She clung to him as he lifted his head. "Agreed?" he asked before lowering his face and kissing her neck.

Her body shuddered at the contact of his lips against her skin. She sighed. "Agreed." He could have asked her to streak down Pennsylvania Avenue and she would have agreed at that point.

The phone rang, splintering the bubble they were ensconced in. She backed out of his hold, keeping her eyes on him as she moved. God, the man was so handsome, his body hard and muscled. The gray in his hair didn't dim the fire inside him, and she could see it smoldering as he looked at her. Amanda reached for the phone and answered it.

"Amanda, I'm not going to be home until late tonight. I'm trying a new process to sort the data I'm getting in. Would you let my dad know? Hopefully, you two will be okay on your own for dinner tonight." Tori rattled off the words.

She smiled as she watched Frank. "Don't worry, Tori, I'll take care of your dad tonight. Be safe at work."

"Thanks. I'll check in at the hospital before I get started."

"We're on our way over now."

"Cool. I'll see you tomorrow, then. It'll be late when I get home."

"Tomorrow. Have a good night." Amanda hung up the phone. "Your daughter won't be home until late. Very late."

Frank smiled. "We should go to the hospital."

Amanda nodded and picked up her purse. "I think we should eat in tonight."

"You're reading my mind." Frank keyed the alarm system and opened the front door.

Amanda exited first and waited for him to lock the door. They walked to the vehicle that Guardian had given Frank to drive. He opened the door and helped her into the massive SUV. She reached over and unlocked his door. He got in and started it.

"Frank?" She glanced at him. He cocked his head in that way of his. The man wasn't much for words, but she'd learned to read his mannerisms. "Did you really want to be *just* friends?"

He chuckled and put the vehicle in Drive. "Nope. Figured it was a place to start, though." He covered her hand and drove with precision through the horrid D.C. traffic.

They entered the ward together. Dixon and Drake were propped up, and Drake was turned on one side so as not to aggravate the burns on his back. "Well, don't you look wonderful?" Amanda walked in and kissed Drake's cheek and then Dixon's. Both of those strawberry blond boys blushed a bright red.

"Doc says we can go in two days. As soon as Drake's through with his course of antibiotics."

"I still have to do the oral meds, but I'll get rid of this." He let the IV tube flop.

Frank nodded. That was good news, but unfortunately, he hedged the fact that his boys would be going home with him around the fact that he'd be leaving Amanda in two days. Bittersweet. "I'll talk to your doctor and arrange a flight back for us. I'll also make sure he gives us some pain management meds for that ride." He stared down Drake, who knew better than to sass him. The man just dipped his head in acknowledgment.

"Wonderful, I'm so happy for your good news, boys. I'll leave you to talk to Frank." Amanda turned and winked at him on the way out.

Frank watched her leave and turned around to the bemused faces of two boys who looked like they wanted to comment. He lifted an eyebrow.

Dixon brought his hands up, gesturing his innocence. "Didn't say a thing. Not going to think a thing. Not going to comment."

"Dixon, you just *did* say something, it is impossible *not* to think, and by saying you're not going to comment, *you just did*." Drake sighed. "Thank God I'm the smart one in this family."

Dixon turned to his brother. "I liked you better when you were drugged out of your mind. Frank, can we get him some more of the good stuff? It was a lot quieter."

Frank chuffed. "You worried about the fact that he wasn't awake like a dog with a bone."

Drake made a swooning sound, "Aww ... D, man, you love me."

Dixon rolled his head and stared at Frank. "I owe you one for that."

Frank dropped his cowboy hat at the foot of Drake's bed and pulled up his chair. Life was never dull with those two.

Dixon cleared his throat. "Have we heard anything about the team?"

Frank pursed his lips and shook his head. "Been a while now."

Drake closed his eyes. "If they haven't found any bodies, they're alive. You can't lose faith."

"Haven't. Just hoping they aren't losing faith, either." He knew every one of Guardian's teams was trained on how to survive in a hostile area. Hell, he and Gabriel had drawn up the training progression and what the minimum training requirements for those serving on the team should be. The necessities wouldn't have changed.

"Skipper won't give up. Getting back to Tori is going to keep him going, and he's going to keep everyone else in line. Him and Joseph." Dixon's statement wasn't open for discussion.

Frank had no idea what Joseph's role was. Seemed from what he'd heard the man was a lone wolf type of operative, which had its merits. He couldn't quite peg why it was troubling him so much to have a single-player deployed in a hostile area.

He and Gabriel had talked numerous times while he was in D.C. They'd gone over ideas for the training complex and worked out the legal aspects of having the facility on the ranch. They hadn't met in person. Gabriel was working like a man possessed to find anything that would lead to his team's recovery. He'd like to have a drink, or hell, even a cup of coffee with his old friend before they traveled back to South Dakota. He'd call again in the morning and see if there was any time in the man's schedule.

"They'll be found," Frank confirmed. Alive or dead, he knew Gabriel wouldn't rest until those boys were home.

Drake nodded his head. "Are you sure you want us to return to South Dakota with you?"

Frank cocked his head at the man-child. "Did I say it?"

Drake smiled. "You did."

"Then I meant it. Need you to get healthy. We have a training annex to plan and build."

"Say what?" Dixon sat up a bit straighter.

"Jacob's idea. Spoke with Gabriel about it. Makes sense. Need a place to rehab those coming off injuries. Someplace out of the way, off the grid, and quiet enough that healing is the only priority. We'll build a small clinic. Strength and stamina training coupled with specialized training as needed. Figured that valley on the other side of the big hill behind the house would be a place to put everything. Out of sight from the road in case someone drives up to the ranch house, far enough away that your operations won't interfere with the ranch's rhythm."

"You're doing this for Guardian?"

"Yup." He and Gabriel had talked about it briefly. His ideas were a bit grander than Jacob's, but Frank could deal with Gabriel's ideas. They made sense, at least to him. He was pretty sure the boys were at a loss as to why he'd allow Guardian to take over eighty acres of land. Didn't matter. They didn't need to know. Yet.

Amanda walked into Jason's room and smiled at her son sitting up, playing solitaire on the rolling metal tray. "How are you feeling today?" She dropped her purse on the chair beside his bed and bent over to kiss his forehead. He was hot. She lifted and narrowed her eyes. "A fever?"

"No. I'm jonesing hard." The cards snapped down onto the metal tray. "I need to get to the weight room. Ride an exercise bike or row or something," Jason muttered as he abused the cards.

She put a hand over his. He stilled and lifted those vivid eyes to look at her. "Did you ask the doctor if you could go for a walk?"

Jason flicked the IV. "With this? Where the hell am I going to go?"

Amanda lifted away from her son and arched an eyebrow.

Jason closed his eyes, breathed in deeply, and slowly let it out. "I'm sorry, Mom."

"You're forgiven." She walked over to the closet and rummaged through the clothes she'd brought for Jason from the Georgetown place. Jacob's sweats. They'd be long enough but probably pretty tight. She grabbed a pair of socks and shoes before going back and pushing away the silver tray. "Put on the sweatpants while I'm finding the doctor. I'll help you with the socks and shoes. With the IV, we aren't going to get a shirt on you, so you'll have to deal with the hospital johnnie."

"Mom, they aren't going to let—"

Amanda turned to her son. "I'm sorry, young man, did I ask for your input?"

"No, ma'am." A tiny smile tweaked at her son's lips.

"Then do as I say." She headed out of the room and went straight to the nurse's desk. "I'm taking my son for a walk. He's going crazy cooped up in that little room and needs to move. What's the closest way to the lovely garden you have in the middle of the hospital?"

The nurse she'd cornered looked up. "Uh ... down this corridor to the elevator, down to the main level. Follow the signs. You can't miss it."

"Thank you." Amanda turned to walk away.

"Ma'am, if you hold on, I can get him a stronger stand with wheels for his IV."

Amanda stopped and turned around. "Thank you, that would be lovely."

"Not a problem. He was in a mood earlier. I'm glad you're taking him for a jaunt. If he gets too tired, just pick up any of the white phones on the wall and dial star twenty-three. That will ring here, and I'll get someone with a wheelchair to come get him."

Amanda glanced at the nurse's name. "Thank you, Janice. I appreciate the help."

"They're our only patients, ma'am. We're going to make sure they're well-cared for. Even if they are a bit grumpy."

Amanda walked with the woman back to Jason's room. "He's really not that grumpy."

The nurse chuckled. "Nobody represents the best person they can be while in the hospital."

"Isn't that the truth," Amanda agreed.

"I'll be back in just a minute. The other stands are down the hall." Janice kept walking when Amanda slowed to go into Jason's room.

Jason was sitting on the bed wearing the sweatpants. "Good. You're ready." She walked over and bent down.

"Mom, you don't have to …"

His voice was raspy from the damage that had been done while he was being held. The marks around his neck were fading, but she'd always see the red gash. "Shush." She put one sock on, then the other. "Foot." She held up the tennis shoe, and Jason shoved his foot into it. She tightened the laces and tied them before doing the same for the other shoe.

"Found it." Janice wheeled an IV stand in the door. "It's old and beat up, but this stand has bigger wheels, and it's made of steel. Not aluminum." The nurse made quick work of moving Jason's IV to the mobile stand. "I'll walk with you to the end of the corridor. Just to make sure you're stable."

Jason rolled his eyes. "I'm not two."

Janice didn't miss a beat. "Good, then don't act like it."

Amanda laughed and covered her mouth. "Janice, I think I like you."

They strolled down the hall, and Jason fared well. Janice hit the button for them. "Star twenty-three if you need a ride back up."

The door shut, and Jason grumped, "As if."

Amanda chuckled. She walked slowly as Jason lost steam down the hall. When she opened the door to the lovely garden area, his mood picked up. "Real sunshine." He wheeled the stand over to a bench and sat down, making sure there was enough room for her.

"The doctor said he's taking this out tomorrow, and if everything is clear with the next round of tests, I'll be free to go home the day after." He closed his eyes and lifted his face to the sun. "God, that feels good."

"Do you want me to book tickets? I'd like you to come home for a while." She wanted to be there to support him while he fought his demons.

Jason shook his head. "I can't … not a plane. Can we drive? I know it's a long way."

"I'd rather drive, actually." She didn't care either way, but she didn't want Jason to feel guilty about a few days in a car.

"Gabriel should be able to provide us with a vehicle."

"I'll call him in the morning." She turned to face him. "What are you going to do? I mean, once you get your life under control."

"Practice law. Contract law. Mississippi could use another lawyer, don't you think?" Jason opened his eyes and looked at her.

She smiled. "I do. Where are you going to practice?"

"I think the Gulf Coast. I don't want to be up in Jackson or Oxford. There's new industry with the casinos and the docks building up." He closed his eyes and dropped his head back again, soaking up the sunshine. "Have you thought about selling the house and downsizing?"

Her eyes popped open in shock. "No, your father built that house. I don't want to let go of it."

"It's too big for you, Mom."

"I have Manny." She shrugged. Manny had been doing handyman work around the place since Chance had been killed. He was a sweet man, and even at seventy, he was competent at fixing things that needed to be mended.

"Manny is older than dirt," Jason countered.

"That's rude." Amanda frowned at her son.

"But true. Just think about it, Mom. We could make sure you're taken care of. You could move here to D.C. or with me on the coast." Jason cracked one eye open. "Thank you for this. I'm exhausted, but I had to get out of that room."

"I know." She patted him on the leg. "I'm not lonely, Jason. I'm not a senior citizen with one leg in a nursing home. I love my home and the memories I have there."

"You're right, Mom. You're young enough to have another relationship, but you won't find anyone back home."

"Sweetheart, I promise you I'm fine, and while I appreciate the dating advice, I'm going to stay where I am." Amanda chuckled when Jason made a sound in his throat. It reminded her of Frank's grunts, each subtly different and specific to a situation.

To say she was excited about tonight, alone with

Frank, was an understatement. She didn't know how they'd pull off being more than friends with so much distance between them. The memory of that kiss, of the chemistry of those kisses, swept over her. Dear lord, it had been forever since she'd felt passion, and yet that was exactly what she felt. Deep, pulling passion for a strong man. A good man who wanted her as much as she wanted him. So what that she was in her fifties and so was he? Life didn't end at forty-nine. Thank God because she felt twenty that afternoon.

"Your face is red. Are you too hot?"

At Jason's questions, she popped her eyes open. "No. No, I'm fine."

"I'm ready to go back." Jason sighed.

"Tired? I can get you a wheelchair." She stood but didn't offer a hand for him to get up because he wouldn't accept it.

"No. I'll be able to sleep when I go back if I do it under my own steam." Jason used the arm and back of the bench to heave himself upright. Amanda waited until he was ready and walked slowly beside him.

"I talked to Tori today. She said there wasn't any news about the others." Jason walked through the door when she pushed it open for him. "Joseph is with them. They'll be all right." She wouldn't let herself believe anything else.

"There should have been some type of signal if they aren't captive," he countered.

"Gabriel told me yesterday that there was no indication of any prisoners in the area. Not that I know how they know that. Stop thinking negatively. They're there, Gabriel and Tori will find them, and they will be coming home. Period." She wasn't going to listen to anything else. Was it a bit of head in the sand? Yes. But thinking anything else was absolutely unacceptable.

**14**
———

"You were quiet on the way home tonight." Frank shut the door behind them and keyed in the alarm code for the Georgetown home that Jacob, Tori, and Jared shared. To tell the truth, he was more than a bit worried that Amanda had changed her mind about being together.

"Was I?" Amanda sighed and put her purse on the hall table by the bowl where Tori usually kept her keys. "Jason raised some concerns about the boys overseas." She smiled wanly at him. "I'm trying to be positive, but it's been a long time. I'm scared for them."

Frank moved into her space and took her in his arms. She tucked up right under his chin like she was made for him. "We keep a positive outlook until we have a reason to believe otherwise." He rubbed her back, and her body relaxed against his.

"I haven't had this in a long time. Someone to share my concerns with. Thank you." She glanced up at him. "I didn't mean to bring the mood down."

He smiled at that. "You didn't. I was worried you'd changed your mind."

She blinked and pulled away. "No. Not at all." Her stomach rumbled, and her eyes widened before she belted out a healthy laugh.

He loved it when she was completely relaxed with him. "We eat, then we see where the night leads us." He placed his cowboy hat on the small table with her purse.

Amanda shook her head and grabbed his hand. "No. We see where the night leads, and then we eat." She tugged him after her, and he gladly followed.

Nerves hit about halfway up the stairs. He wanted to be with her, lord knew he did, and his body was charged and ready, but it had been a while since he'd been with a lady. A long while. *Make it all about her*. He smiled as they reached the top of the stairs. He'd have no problem doing that.

Amanda opened the door to the bedroom where she'd been sleeping, and they both stepped in. "I don't know why I feel like a schoolgirl sneaking her boyfriend up to her room."

Frank chuckled. "I won't tell if you won't."

Amanda reached up and unsnapped the top fastener on his shirt. "Never." She leaned forward and kissed his chest.

*Time to take charge, Marshall.*

He unfastened the pin that held the scarf around her neck. The neckline plunged, exposing the rounded swell of her breasts. He lowered for a kiss as he unfastened the long zipper that ran from her neck to the middle of her nicely rounded ass. The material bunched, and he slid his hands along the softness of her back before he removed the dress from her shoulders. It slipped to her feet.

"Beautiful." He held her hand as she stepped out of the dress. Her lacy white bra and panties showcased her soft curves and long expanses of skin covering a remarkably fit body.

"I'm a long way from beautiful." She placed her hand over her stomach. The faint silver lines from pregnancies were noticeable.

He reached down and removed her hand, putting it to his mouth and kissing it. "We've lived a life, Amanda. Our scars make us who we are. I'm attracted to you. All of you. The beauty I see is deeper than the barrier of your skin. Don't belittle yourself with doubt. You are beautiful to me. All of you."

Her breath caught before she smiled and moved to unfasten another snap on his shirt. "You know, for a man of few words, you say the most amazing things."

He smiled and let her unfasten his shirt. He pulled it off and was pretty damn proud of her response. She ran her hands over his chest, and his pecs jumped from the excitement of her touch.

"Amazing." She looked up at him. "Your body is amazing."

"No more than yours." Frank dropped for a kiss. One hand unhooked her bra as the other found its way underneath the lacy cups. Her nipples were hard, and they tightened even more under his touch. He backed them to the king-size bed, and when he felt her legs hit the soft border, he lowered her before he stood back up and undressed.

He toed off his boots as he unbuckled his belt and unfastened his jeans. Amanda sat up in bed and tossed the bra to the floor. She shimmied out of her panties as he dropped his jeans.

"God, you're magnificent," she said.

Amanda's eyes on him did nothing but incite the

fire inside him. He kneed onto the bed and moved over her. "If you could only see what I see." He took her mouth in a kiss as he lowered over her body. She moved so he could settle between her legs. He took his time discovering her body. The feel of her hands on him and the scrape of fingernails on his arms or back when he found a place that excited her were all mapped in his mind. He lifted over her after kissing every inch of her, tasting her and memorizing her responses. "Are you ready?" he whispered as he leaned down for a kiss.

When he lifted away, she smiled and nodded. "Yes. Come inside me, Frank."

He nudged his way in. Her hot, wet core around his shaft was the most remarkable sensation. He dropped his head to her shoulder.

"You're so big." She panted beneath him.

He pulled away. "Do you need—"

"No. Stay. God, stay. So good." She cupped his face and pulled him down for a kiss. Who was he to deny her? She opened for him, and his tongue danced with hers as he moved within her. The intimacy and sensations were powerful, and God, he'd never felt this with Elizabeth. The need, the want on her end.

Amanda's body moved under him. She touched

him, urged him on, rose to meet his thrusts, reciprocated his kisses, and became one with him. He reached between them and massaged her. Amanda's body jumped and bucked as they rode each other to the top of that mountain. He closed his eyes, praying he'd be able to wait until ...

When she bowed and released, he let himself go and came harder than he'd ever done before. He was a wash of sweat above her.

She opened her eyes and smiled widely at him. "Thank you."

He blinked and then laughed. "I think I should be saying that." He dropped to her side, and she rolled with him.

"No. Believe me, that orgasm was well worth me thanking you."

He laughed. "Ditto."

Amanda tucked herself next to him. "I thought I'd never do this again."

He stroked her hair. "Know that feeling."

"Is it wrong to be so happy when the boys are in harm's way?" She ran her fingers through the hair on his chest.

"Can't be." He knew what she meant. They were taking pleasure when the boys were in danger, or worse, injured or captured. "Can't be wrong when it feels this way between us." He restated it because he firmly believed it. He wouldn't let guilt separate him from this woman.

Amanda's stomach rumbled, and she laughed. "I didn't eat lunch today. I'll go down and make something for us." She rolled and sat up.

He lifted up on his elbows. "I'll come with you." Being in bed while she was working in the kitchen didn't sit well with him.

Amanda glanced at the clock. "It's only eight. Do you think Tori will be home soon?"

Frank shook his head. "If she said she'd be late, she's going to work."

Amanda's face split into a massive grin. "Good." She stood up, reached for his shirt, and put it on. The tail reached about mid-thigh. Her long black hair fell over her shoulders. God, she was a beautiful sight. "I may steal this shirt from you."

He grabbed his briefs and looked over his shoulder at her. "Why's that?"

"Because I want to have something of yours when you're not with me. Does that make me weird?"

He shook his head. "Nope." She smiled and walked out the door. Frank put on his jeans. Hell, she could have his entire suitcase if she wanted it.

## Frank

"Hey, Daddy. Did you have a good night?"

Frank looked up from pouring his coffee as Tori came into the kitchen. "I did." An understatement of gigantic proportions, if ever there was one. "Your new tactic work?"

Tori sighed and rubbed her forehead. "No. I was snatching for straws."

"You'll figure it out, Tori. You're overlooking something, looking at it wrong. Give yourself the grace to figure it out."

"But they've been missing for so long."

"And you know in your heart they are going to come home." He handed her the coffee he'd just poured and pulled down another cup.

"I do," she whispered and blew on the coffee. "How are the boys?"

"Everyone should be going home Friday. I'll call Gabriel today and get our transportation sorted."

Tori nodded. "Jason, too?"

"Yes," Amanda said as she floated through the door. She wore a pair of jeans and a T-shirt and had her hair pulled up into a high ponytail.

*Good lord, she looks thirty if she looks a day.*

"Good, I'm so glad he can start his recovery

again." Tori opened the refrigerator and looked into it as Frank passed Amanda the second cup of coffee he'd poured. She winked at him and accepted it, standing near him, leaning against the countertop.

"Eggs?" Tori pulled the carton out of the fridge.

"I'll cook. You sit down with your father. Over easy on toast with some sausage?" Amanda asked as she took the eggs from Tori.

"I don't mind," Tori began, but Amanda waved her off.

"You're working; I'm visiting."

"Eggs sound good to me." Frank poured himself a cup and took a sip. Worth the wait.

"Thank you, Amanda. Are you and Jason going to fly back to ... Heck, where would you fly into?"

"We could go into Gulfport or New Orleans, but Jason doesn't want to fly. He has issues with being confined right now."

Tori nodded and sighed. "I read the report. They kept him in a small cage. Bound."

Amanda stopped moving for a moment, and Frank saw the wince that crossed her face. Obviously, her son hadn't told her that. He cleared his throat. Tori looked at him, and he shook his head slightly. She looked perplexed until he nodded toward Amanda. Tori's eyes widened, and she mouthed the word, *Shit*. He lifted an eyebrow, and she rolled her eyes. "Sorry."

"What, dear?" Amanda asked from near the range.

"Nothing. Did you two go out to dinner last night?"

"No, we stayed in." Amanda nodded to the dishes in the strainer. "I made dinner here. Neither of us wanted to deal with the crush of the D.C. traffic."

"I can't say as I blame you." Tori rolled her shoulders. "So, you just hung out?"

"We visited." Frank nodded. They'd done that and more. He lifted his cup to his mouth to prevent his stupid smile from showing. Amanda had taken over his DNA so much so that she was about all he could think about. That woman was the fire in his veins, and damned if he didn't want to burn to death.

"Good, I'm so glad you two are friends." Tori sighed and put her cup on the table. "Now, if we can just get Jacob, Joseph, and Jared home."

"We will," Amanda confirmed as she buttered toast.

Tori nodded, but Frank saw the doubt in her eyes. Damn it. She couldn't give up. "Have faith in your abilities, Victoria." He stared at her as she lifted her eyes from the coffee cup.

"Yeah. I do. I'm just tired. Amanda, I'm just going to have toast. My stomach is a bit queasy. I must've had too much coffee yesterday and not enough water."

"Oh, sure." Amanda brought a piece of toast over to the table.

Tori smiled at her mother-in-law. "Thank you."

Frank watched his daughter pick at the toast without eating any of it. He needed to talk to Gabriel. She was looking tired. Maybe she needed a forced stand-down to recharge and look at the problem with fresh eyes.

## 15

Amanda waited by the hostess stand. Frank's hand on her back was a comfort she'd long forgotten. The feel of a man standing protectively beside her was exhilarating. Did she need him to protect her? No, she was very adept at taking care of herself, but when Chance had been alive, she'd never thought twice about the protective stance he always took. Just like Frank. They were similar in a lot of ways, her late husband and Frank, and at the same time, completely different. Chance was a talker and a dreamer. They'd worked hard and scraped and saved after he left his family back east. Life was never easy for them, with so many mouths to feed, but there was an abundance of love.

"This way." Amanda moved forward, following the hostess. Frank's hand fell from her waist, and the lack of warmth was noticeable. O'Malley's was Justin's restaurant. Well, some of the boys had gone in with him on it. It was a lovely steakhouse. She'd recommended it when Frank suggested lunch with Gabriel.

Gabriel hadn't arrived, but the hostess seated them at a semi-secluded table near a window that looked out into the garden area where people who waited to get in could wander or sit on any of the many benches located among the greenery.

"Mr. King has already ordered luncheon for you as his guests. The chef will be with you shortly." The hostess left, and a waiter stepped up.

"Good afternoon. I'm Elan, your lead server today. Mr. King has suggested the wines to accompany your luncheon, and the chef has created a meal around them. Mr. King sends his apologies that he won't be here today. Business has called him elsewhere. May I proceed?"

A tug at the corner of Frank's lips told her he was amused at the service. She'd experienced the preferential treatment several times but still worried if she was using the right fork. She was a country girl through and through. Chance had been raised in an influential family on the east coast and knew which fork was for what. She'd learned enough not to embarrass herself. "Thank you, that would be lovely, but we're waiting for one more."

"Two, actually." She turned at Gabriel's voice behind her. Frank stood up and shook Gabriel's hand. "This is my wife, Anna. I thought since she hadn't seen me except for a couple glimpses in the last month, we could turn this lunch into a proof of life check for her as well."

Frank shook Anna's hand. "Gabriel usually jokes about how much he's away, but not this time. He's been at work more than he's been home since the trouble overseas. Frank, it's good to meet you finally. Amanda, I've wanted to meet you for so long." Anna sat beside her as the waitstaff flew into action and placed another setting at the table.

"Gabriel has been a godsend while Jason and the twins have been hospitalized." Amanda liked Anna immediately. The woman had an air of honesty around her. Fake people moved in her children's circle, and it took seconds to sense the veneer of appearance that dripped off people who wanted to be seen and noticed. Anna didn't give that vibe off at all.

"How are they? I haven't been to the hospital

since the first day they arrived. Gabriel felt it was better to let family check in on them. Even though I'm a nurse." She turned her head and stared at her husband as she spoke.

Gabriel stopped with his water glass halfway to his lips. "They have nurses."

Anna rolled her eyes. "Not my point. So, how are they doing?" Anna spun and asked again.

"They're going to be discharged on Friday. The twins will go back to South Dakota with Frank, and I'll take Jason home with me to Mississippi."

"I'll arrange transportation. Two flights. We can be ready to leave as soon as you are."

Frank shook his head. "Can you arrange a driver and a vehicle for Jason and Amanda? He's not ready to be confined in a small space yet."

Gabriel blinked and looked at Amanda. "Of course. I'll arrange the driver and hotels. It's at least a two-day trip."

Amanda put her hand on Frank's arm. "I can drive."

"I'd feel better if you didn't have to drive that far." He put his hand over hers.

She smiled up at him. "Thank you."

Anna leaned back. "How long has this been

going on?" She smiled brightly. "And can I say, 'Yay?' I mean, we have zero couples as friends."

"My fault." Gabriel nodded to the waiter, who began the service.

"No one's fault," Anna countered. "Just the life we lead." She turned to Amanda. "Is this thing between you new?"

Frank grunted, and Gabriel laughed.

"What was that?" Anna laughed, too.

"I believe that was Frank saying he doesn't want to talk about their relationship." Gabriel chuckled and tasted the wine that the server poured into his glass. He nodded at the server.

Amanda shook her head. "It's very new, and we haven't told the children. We thought we'd like to see where it goes before we mix our adult children into it."

His parents had taught him to keep his personal life private, and he did. He was a leftover from a different age. He didn't understand how people went online and shared the most intimate details of their lives. People around him got that message loud and clear, and he wouldn't change the way they perceived him. It was good to have your boundaries respected.

"Gosh, that makes so much sense." Anna took a sip of her wine and cringed.

Gabriel lifted his hand and summoned the waiter. "I'll need ice cubes for my wife. Also, only red wine."

The server blinked but nodded his understanding and backed away. "I've talked to Jason." Gabriel leaned forward. "He told me he's leaving Guardian, but I've enticed him to remain as my private lawyer. I'm not ready for him to cut ties."

Amanda nodded her head. "We can't keep them all with Guardian. He has to find a balance first. Regain confidence in his sobriety, and really, Gabriel, it isn't your responsibility any longer. They're adults."

Gabriel placed an ice cube in his wife's glass and stirred the wine until it was chilled. "I know. But I made Chance a promise. I told him I'd take care of them and you." He flicked a quick look in Frank's direction. "You're in good hands with this one."

"Thanks." Frank's droll reply made all of them laugh.

"Any word on the boys overseas?" Amanda had the urgent feeling that the more time passed, the harder it would be to locate them. Frank put his hand over hers.

"No. But we're taking that as good news. If we had intelligence about them, that would mean they were in hostile hands." Gabriel shrugged. "I'm not to the point of giving up."

"Speaking of reaching a point ..." Frank leaned forward. "Tori needs a break. She's working herself to death. She needs time off to refresh and then look at the problem. Sometimes you can't see the forest for the trees."

"They all need to do that." Anna looked at her husband. "But some are more pig-headed than others."

Gabriel lifted an eyebrow. "Are you referring to anyone in particular, my love?"

Anna snorted. "You and Jewell."

Gabriel nodded. "She's not left the building since they went missing except to go to the hospital."

"Both of them need to be sent home for a day." Frank nodded. "Can't work when you're past exhausted."

Gabriel nodded. "I agree. I'll see what I can do." A convoy of waiters descended with their plates. The appetizers under the glass-domed plates were exquisite.

After the plates were cleared, Anna nodded

toward Amanda. "I'm going to make a run to the back. You need to?"

Amanda smiled. Such a typical girl thing. "Sure." Both Gabriel and Frank stood and pulled their chairs out for them. She smiled up at Frank. Her heart, although broken by the plight of her boys, was also full. She'd have to wrestle that feeling to the ground as they drove home to Mississippi.

∽

"I've known Amanda for a long time now." Gabriel leaned forward.

Frank cocked his head and stared at his friend. "Warning me off?"

Gabriel snorted. "Hell, no. Just wanted you to know she's an amazing person. She raised those kids with no help."

"Heard there was a life insurance policy. When did that policy start?" Frank took a drink of the wine. It wasn't bad.

"After Chance died. I've made sure she was taken care of and that the kids stayed out of trouble, which, for some of them, has been an effort," Gabriel chuckled before leaning forward. "She raised eight kids. She's strong. Worthy of you."

Frank wiped his mouth with his napkin. "The question is, am I worthy of her?"

"I think you two together make more sense than any other match I've ever witnessed. Well, except Anna and me. Perfection is hard to duplicate. When this is over, the four of us need to take some time and relax. Can you get away from the ranch for a long weekend?"

Frank nodded. He could. Keelee was more than capable of running things while he was gone. She was doing it now with their hand Danny, Aunt Betty, and the Koehlers helping out. There were days they were stretched tight, but for a ranch the size of his, they had operations streamlined. "Like that. I'm figuring on making trips to Mississippi. Amanda doesn't want to let the kids know. I'm in line with that type of thinking. My private life isn't open for discussion." He leveled a look at Gabriel.

Gabriel laughed and lifted his hands. "I get the message. Just think the two of you are good. Before the ladies get back, we've got the contract for the land drafted. You'll have the only copy. I don't want anything that ties this organization or me to the ranch. As we grow, the negative side of the world becomes more obvious. I'm taking precautions with my family. I'd like to make sure we do the same with yours and Amanda's."

Frank nodded. "Builders?"

"Will be local and people you can trust. When we get to the special infrastructure, I'll fly in a vetted team, but that will be some time down the road. I'll send out the list I'm considering, but I need your input. You'll be there, and I won't be. I need your take on it."

"I'll make sure it'll work." He wouldn't let something half-assed go up. But he had other things on his mind. "Let's cut through the cow dung. What are the chances those boys are gone?"

Gabriel glanced toward the bathroom. "Fifty-fifty. I wasn't lying. There isn't any information that leads me to believe the hostiles have them. If they were dead, we'd have a video desecrating their bodies or making a statement. There's nothing. I think they're holding tight until they can make a run for it."

"To where?"

Gabriel shook his head. "That's just it. I don't know, and the buildup of personnel in that area would lead me to believe if we don't find them soon, the hostiles will."

Frank could see the ladies laughing as they approached. "Anything I can do?"

Gabriel stood, and as he did, he said, "Pray."

Frank stood and pulled the chair out for Amanda. He could do that, and he would.

## 16

*Present Day, Marshall Ranch, South Dakota:*

"That's why you forced Tori and me to leave for the weekend?" Jewell asked before she popped a marshmallow into her mouth.

Gabriel nodded. "Well, that, and you needed to shower."

Zane chuckled, and Jewell frowned at her husband. "Excuse me?"

"Face it, babe, you can forget what day it is if you get buried in a project. No doubt you were up to your eyeballs in gathering data to help your brothers." Zane took the marshmallow bag, took out four big fluffy puffs of sugar, and handed them to her. He tossed the others back toward the fire. Jade was toasting a skewer full now. Jillian and Drake were sitting on the couch where she and Nic had been sitting.

"She used to resemble that remark," Jacob said.

"Until you showed up. And yes, we realize we took advantage of her," Jason agreed.

"Meh, y'all were worth it." Jewell waved them away.

"Drake had to stay. His blood work showed the infection wasn't under control. Amanda left with Jason about a week before we headed back to South Dakota." Frank held his wife's hand. They'd talked on the phone just about every night during that time. Jason had a hard go of things but got plugged into an NA meeting and started walking on the treadmill. The local doctor had advised against doing anything more strenuous for at least a month. The man logged more hours on the treadmill than one would think humanly possible.

"Tori found us a few days after you left, Amanda." Jacob put his arm around his wife and kissed her temple. Tori turned and smiled up at him. "Don't forget, I found Karla Miller first."

Jacob groaned and dropped his head back on the couch. Joseph guffawed and nearly choked on his drink. Ember whapped him on the back. "That's what you get for laughing."

"Karla?" Jade perked up real fast with that one.

"Do tell," Jillian said around a mouth full of s'mores.

"Wait, isn't Karla Miller a runway model?" Keelee sat up. "I watched a special of that modeling superstar show, and she was the guest judge. Really pretty with red hair?"

"Keelee, please don't help," Jacob groaned.

"Beautiful, isn't she? She had the combination to the alarm panel and a key to the house."

Tori took a drink of her water as Keelee blinked and squeaked, "Say what now?"

"She was an occasional hookup." Jacob looked at Tori, pleading with her. "You know that."

Tori couldn't keep a stern face and laughed. "I do. I still like to see you squirm."

Mike laughed, and Taty elbowed him. "What? It's funny." He rubbed his stomach. "Brutal."

"It's the Russian in me." Taty handed him her glass. "I need another drink, please." She turned to look at Amanda. "How long until you two got married?" Mike kissed Taty and hopped to his feet to get her a drink from the bar.

Amanda glanced over at Frank. "Two years."

"You guys were dating when we had Talon's christening here?" Jacob asked.

Amanda smiled. "More than dating."

"Mom!" The collective groan rattled the rafters. Frank laughed along with Gabriel, Anna, and Amanda. "What?" She motioned to the four of them sitting on the couch. "We're not dead. You'll be lucky to have what we have when your children are your age."

"La la la la la. Not listening." Jewell plugged her ears.

"See, I kept telling you these guys let their freak flag wave," Jade interjected.

"Jade!" The clamor rose again. Leave it to the wild one to light everyone's wick just to watch the explosion.

Jared and Christian exchanged places with Nic and Jade. "How did you do that without any of us finding out?" Jared asked as he shoved marshmallows onto the end of his skewer.

Frank shifted and stood. "Would you like a drink?"

She nodded. "Yes, please."

He glanced at Anna and Gabriel. "I've got ours."

"You can talk while you fix your drinks, Dad," Keelee suggested.

He grunted. "I had a daughter who was hell-bent on not seeing anything that was happening on the ranch. For me, it was easy."

"Excuse me?" Keelee sounded offended at his comment.

He looked at her. "You were so messed up because of this guy that you didn't notice anything happening outside of that focus."

Keelee blinked and then agreed, "I was rather distracted."

"Rather," Frank parroted. He poured his drink and then mixed one for Amanda. "I spent at least one long weekend a month with Amanda at her house."

"And we all went on a cruise together." Anna nodded.

"And then there was that week in Colorado," Gabriel added.

"Holy hell. Where were we?" Jason shook his head.

"Living your lives, where you should have been. I was at the house when Ember called for Joseph."

"You were?" Ember asked.

. . .

FIFTEEN YEARS AGO, *Amanda's Mississippi Home:*

"ARE YOU SURE?" Amanda stared up the ladder at the bottom of Frank's boots.

"Yup. Going to have to replace it." He started down the ladder, and she moved out of the way, still holding on to the metal ladder to steady it. "When was the last time you put new shingles on the house?"

Amanda blinked and looked up. "I've never re-shingled it."

Frank gave her a look before he shook his head. "Then it's high time. Where's the phone book? I'll call and get some quotes. You've got hurricane season coming up."

"But I'm not on the coast."

"Doesn't matter. You have a small leak now. Any amount of wind and rain and you'll have a real problem on your hands." He dropped down and gave her a kiss. "I'll take care of it."

"Frank, honey, you can't keep paying for the repairs on my house." He'd practically rebuilt the thing from the inside out. Every time he came down, they did some little project for the house. It was wonderful, but ... "I can pay to get it fixed."

"Know it. Don't care." He walked into the kitchen and pulled open the junk drawer that held her phone book.

The phone on the wall rang. "Seriously, I can do it."

"Know it."

She rolled her eyes. That was Frank's way of saying it wasn't going to happen. The phone rang again. She popped over and picked it up. "Hello?"

"Hi, Mrs. King, this is Ember Harris. I know this must be a surprise, but I was wondering if you could give me Joseph's telephone number. I'm in the process of moving, and I seem to have misplaced it."

She gasped, and Frank's eyes were on her in an instant. She waved him off. *Ember Harris.* She was such a wonderful young lady. But, my, it had been a hot minute, as the kids said, since she'd talked to the woman. "Ember! Honey, how have you been? It's been forever since you called. Tell me, how are you doing? You said you are moving? Where are you going?"

Ember's polite reply was hesitant. "Yes, ma'am, I'm sorry for not calling sooner, but working sixty to seventy hours a week at the trauma center didn't leave me much time to visit."

That would be true. The woman was an emergency room doctor. Of all the professions, it amazed her that the sweet young lady had chosen that one. "Well, you're forgiven since you called now, dear. Where are you moving to?" Amanda sat down at the table across from Frank. Such a pleasant surprise.

"Ummm ... I don't know yet? I'm taking an extended vacation, and I'm going to do some traveling. I went from high school to college to med school and then straight to work. I never took any time for myself, so ..."

Amanda nodded. She got it. Chance was the same way, except he never took time for himself. Her children were just as driven as her late husband had been. "So now you're taking care of yourself. I'm so happy for you, dear. Can I expect to see you while you're on vacation?"

"Ah, you know, Mississippi isn't on my list, but who knows, I may just show up one day."

Amanda smiled. Although she knew the comment was a polite blow-off, she'd love to see Ember again. "I'd love that, dear. You know you're always welcome here. You're practically a member of the family."

"Yes, ma'am, thank you. Ahh ... Mrs. King, I can't find Joey's telephone number. Would you happen to have a way I can get in touch with him? It's kind of important that I talk to him right away."

And the conversation just tripped into dangerous territory. She glanced at Frank, who was writing down telephone numbers. "Ember, honey, are you in trouble?"

Frank's head snapped up. Amanda covered the receiver. "She wants Joseph's number." Frank's brow creased, and he tipped his head. Ember was silent, so she was in trouble. Amanda drew a breath and sighed it out. "Okay, sweetheart, I'm giving you his emergency contact number. Leave a message and give him a number to call you back. I don't know if he's in the country or overseas, but he'll call you as soon as he gets your message. It could take a couple days or longer. Maybe you should call Jacob or Jared? They're in the States, and they could help you if you're in trouble. If you need a lawyer, Jason has an office here in town." Amanda stood and went to her purse, where she pulled out the cell phone she rarely used. She flicked through it to get Joseph's emergency contact number.

"No, ma'am, I don't need a lawyer. I really just

need to talk to Joey. If he doesn't call me back soon, maybe I'll ask for Jared's number. Okay?"

So it was bad trouble. Dear lord, she prayed Joseph would see the call. "All right, dear. I won't pry. Lord knows I want to, but I won't. Here's the number." She rattled off the number for Ember, and they ended the call shortly after.

"Sounds like the young lady is in need of help." Frank leaned back in his chair and extended a hand to her.

She took it and sat down on his lap. "If Joseph is in the States, he'll move the devil out of hell to help her. He was very much in love with her when they were growing up. I don't know what happened between them."

"Life," Frank said and rested his chin on her shoulder. "Let it go. If they need our help, they'll ask."

"I know. I know." She sighed and relaxed back into him. "Maybe you should stop worrying about my roof for now."

"Yeah? Why's that?" Frank asked.

"I think you should worry about other things right now." She moved her hips against him. A low laugh tickled the back of her neck.

"I'll take care of other things, but I will get your roof fixed."

Amanda made a noncommittal sound. She knew how to distract her man. She'd occupy his time, and then she'd get the quotes to fix the roof.

## 17

*Present Day, Marshall Ranch, South Dakota:*

"So, how did Gabriel and the rest of them distract you when Joey's event happened?" Ember's question stilled the crowd.

Gabriel shook his head. "It wasn't my idea." He pointed at Joseph. "It was his. He wanted to ensure Amanda was out of the country and away from any news sources. We also had to make sure Ember wasn't tracked or followed."

Joseph nodded. "It was necessary." He looked at

Amanda. "I'd do it again, Mom. I had to protect those closest to me in case things didn't work out."

"You know how I felt about being lied to." Ember crossed her arms. "I'm still mad."

Joseph huffed. "You clocked me."

"Damn right I did. I'd do it again." His wife turned to look at him. "We are a *team*."

"Now." Joseph nodded. "*Now*. Then, it wasn't for me or you to decide. I couldn't risk anyone coming after you."

Amanda sighed. Frank felt the tension in her shoulders, though, as she spoke, "I appreciate you thought you had to do what you did, but I would prefer you don't do that again. Like your wife, I won't slip to the floor in a swoon, either."

Taty nodded. "She's tough. Just think back six months. She's got the fortitude to be a Guardian."

Amanda smiled at Taty. "Thank you."

"Okay, no debate on that, but what did they do to distract you?" Jillian licked chocolate from her fingers.

"Well, we didn't suffer," Anna laughed. "Our husbands flew us to a private island in the Bahamas. No internet, no cell phones, and nothing but blue skies, cool breezes, sun, and sand."

Amanda sighed. "The Bahamas. It was heavenly." She sent Frank a sideways look, and he nodded. "It's where Frank asked me to marry him."

"What?" Jade sat up. "How? How did it happen? Come on, dish." She moved to sit closer, but Nic pulled her down beside him.

"Babe, this is their story. They'll tell you when they're ready."

Jade let out an exasperated breath. "Whatever."

Frank shook his head. The wild one was worse than some of his grandchildren. Impatient and demanding, but Nic seemed to have a handle on her.

He took a sip of his drink. "We were there for a week before we flew to Aruba, to Joseph and Ember's wedding."

"A week?" Keelee cocked her head and narrowed her eyes. "Ohhh ... The trip to Arizona to buy the new bulls." She snorted. "That's why the new stock never materialized."

Frank chuckled. "As I said, your head was elsewhere." He pointed his finger at Adam.

His son-in-law lifted his drink. "Guilty."

"Yeah, but come on, tell us ..."

Jade's whine made Frank laugh. "It wasn't that special."

"Yes, it was." Amanda smiled at him with the

same smile she'd given him that night. She was still as beautiful as she was the day he'd met her.

~

*Fifteen years ago, the Bahamas:*

"What do you and Amanda have planned for the evening?" Gabriel stretched out on the lounger by the pool. The women had gone inside to fix a pitcher of fruity drinks. Frank lifted a tumbler of the good stuff. He wasn't much for sitting on his ass and doing nothing, but the island they were on could make him change his mind. He and Amanda had explored every inch of the place, and he'd held the shells and sea glass she'd collected on their journeys. She had a clear decanter full of small shells and blue-green sea glass. It was kinda pretty if you liked that type of thing, and she did.

"Same stuff, different day. Walk on the beach after dinner, then back to the bungalow. Heard anything from Joseph?" He glanced toward the kitchen to make sure Amanda and Anna were still occupied.

"No updates, which is a good thing. We're monitoring all sources. I think it worked." Gabriel shook his head. "I pray it does. Mike gave Ember the packet, and my understanding is no one is sure if she's going to do as Joseph asked."

"She's one strong-willed filly. Has to be to put up with Joseph, though." Frank looked out to the green-blue expanse of the ocean view in front of him. "He's getting out of that line of work completely, right?" Gabriel had filled him in on the who's and why's of the situation.

"Yup. Understand they'll be at the ranch to help Maliki. At least, that's what Joseph was intending. Ember may veto that. Hell, she might not even go to Aruba." Gabriel shook his head. "I don't know what he'll do if she doesn't."

"He'll find her." There wasn't a doubt in his ex-military mind that Joseph would scour the globe for that woman. He loved her that much.

"True." Gabriel nodded. "Speaking of which, Anna and I are going to fly to Europe in a couple months. Do you and Amanda want to try to sneak away with us?"

"February in Europe? Why?" He turned to look at his friend.

"Valentine's Day in Italy. Terni, to be exact. After that, I want to take her to the Venice Carnival." He shrugged. "That is if things settle down. I don't tell her about my plans in case they don't pan out. She deserves better."

"You'd need to turn the reins over to someone else. Can you let someone else drive your wagon?" He doubted it. Guardian was in Gabriel's DNA.

"Been thinking hard about that. I believe I have the right person in mind. The stars need to align. Then I need to do some convincing." Gabriel chuckled. "I'm told I'm pretty convincing when I want to be."

Frank grunted. No doubt about that. "Your work is hard on her?" Frank nodded toward the kitchen, where he could hear Amanda and Anna laughing.

"It is. The time alone is the hardest, she tells me. She doesn't complain, mind you, but I want to spend my time with her, not have a hit-and-miss relationship. There are only so many days given to us. You know what I mean?"

He nodded as Gabriel's words sank in and found fertile ground. He was tired of the hit-and-miss relationship, too. He wanted Amanda with him at the ranch and by his side where she belonged. She wasn't a city girl, and she'd been to the ranch and loved it. He took another drink of his bourbon. Why were they waiting? A perfect time to tell the kids? Hell, with the lot they had, that would never happen. Never. He swished his drink around the insulated tumbler. No, there was no good reason to put their happiness on the back burner.

The women exited the kitchen laughing. "Gabriel, I think Trey is going to have a heart attack. He didn't want us to make our own drinks."

Frank didn't doubt it. The man was a nervous thing when anyone went into the kitchen. Amanda came and sat down next to him. "He was vibrating so bad I thought he was going to explode by the time we were done touching his equipment."

Anna's eyes went wide, and she busted out in laughter. She pointed to Amanda and laughed. "I can't believe you just said that."

Amanda jerked back a bit. "What? What ... Oh, my God, Anna! I would never!" Frank laughed as Amanda sputtered like an old truck with water in the gas tank. "Frank, that wasn't what I meant."

He couldn't help it; he laughed harder, which made Anna snort and throw back her head, laughing harder, too. Then Gabriel, who'd been trying not to laugh, joined in. Frank put down his drink, took Amanda's icy yellow drink, and set it beside his before he wrapped his arms around her. She covered her face and groaned, "I didn't mean it that way," her embarrassment hitting mortification level.

But all he could do was laugh and nod. "I know."

~

Amanda squeezed his hand as they walked alongside the surf on the white, sandy beach. The moon reflected off the water and illuminated the shoreline. The small solar lights along the footpaths twinkled like fireflies inland. It was a beautiful night, and the air was cool and sweet. A good place, that island. "You've been quiet tonight. Is everything all right?" Amanda's concern jerked him out of his contemplation.

"According to most, I don't talk much at all." Frank chuckled. It was true, he didn't use unnecessary words, but he and Amanda had spent hours talking about everything under the stars. He couldn't remember talking to anyone as much as he spoke to her. Which was another reason he was so sure he needed to ask her to marry him.

"I know better. Besides, one of your grunts could be a dissertation for some."

He stopped walking and pulled her into his arms. Her soft white skirt fluttered in the air as the breeze off the water blew around them. "I got something to say tonight."

Amanda smiled up at him. "More than one grunt?"

"Couple." He winked at her. "I was talking to Gabriel today, and he said something that made me realize as a couple, we've made a horrible mistake."

Amanda blinked at him, and her face fell. "What?"

She attempted to pull away from his embrace, but he locked his arms around her. "We have. We've put our lives on hold because of our children and their drama. Now, that's not to say what's happening in their lives isn't important, but we're important, too."

Amanda narrowed her eyes. "I'm trying to understand what you're saying. Honest, I am, but where is the mistake?"

"Amanda, I want you by my side for the rest of my life. We have a love I've never experienced. A connection that is soul-deep. I'm not the man Chance was, and I would never attempt to replace him in your or the children's life. I want you to marry me. Be my wife, my life partner. Be with me during the ups and downs. Stand beside me as my wife as we get old."

Amanda stared up at him. He could see the shimmer of tears in her eyes. "Frank, Chance is long gone. I will always love him, but I thank God for every moment we share together. I've been blessed to love two men in my lifetime. I love you, Frank, in a way I didn't love Chance. Maybe we would have grown to this place, but I'll never know, and I can't care because I'm here with you now. I'll marry you."

He kissed her until he couldn't breathe. She tucked in under his chin, and he hugged her tight. "Tomorrow."

She jerked back, hitting his chin with the top of her head. "Ouch." She rubbed the back of her head as he figured out if he had a tongue left. "Could have done without that." He chuckled.

"Sorry. We can't get married tomorrow." She rubbed her head. "Can we?"

"Bahamas don't make you wait." Yeah, he still had a tongue, although he might have bitten through it.

Amanda stopped rubbing the back of her head and snapped her head in his direction. "Wait, how do you know that?"

"I had Trey make some calls. Figured you wouldn't be hanging around him anymore today, so there was no worry he'd let something slip."

Amanda rolled her eyes. "I did not mean what I said the way Anna took it."

Frank smiled. "It was still funny."

She shoved him lightly on his chest. "Stop."

"All right, I won't mention it again. But I can't promise Anna won't bring it up." Amanda dropped her head to his chest and groaned.

"So, we're going to do this?" She sighed against him.

"Seems about right." Frank nodded. It seemed perfect to him.

"Anna and Gabriel can be our witnesses." She moved carefully and didn't knock his chin this time as she looked up at him.

"Figured that would work since we have to take his boat to another island."

Amanda tipped her head back and forth. "Well, there is that. When do we tell the children? They don't even know we've been seeing each other." Amanda pulled her bottom lip between her teeth.

"We'll figure out the details after we get married." He didn't think the kids would have too much of an issue with their relationship. And if they did? It was their problem, not his and Amanda's.

He walked his fiancée back to their bungalow. The patio doors stood open to the ocean and surf. A soft glow from the inside set his internal "what the hell" meter on edge. As they approached, he saw the reason.

The entire bungalow glowed with tall stacks of white candles. Trey had been busy because Frank sure as heck didn't think to ask for the extras. There was a silver bucket with champagne, chocolate-covered strawberries, and rose petals scattered on the white sheets of the bed. In the middle were two swans made from towels with rose petals surrounding them shaped in a heart. Well, Trey had made him look damn good, hadn't he? He was going to make sure Trey got a raise.

"Oh, Frank, it's beautiful," Amanda said and turned into his arms.

"Yes, you are." He lowered for a kiss and nudged them back toward the bed. Their clothes disappeared in a slow, sensual dance. Amanda's sunkissed skin was soft under his touch. When he moved over her, she shook her head and pushed his shoulder. He dropped to the bed, and she straddled him, her magnificent body a sight to behold. "God, you're beautiful." He ran his hands up her thighs to her hips.

"No, I'm average, nothing special. Love has made you blind." She bent down to kiss him.

"Then I never want to see again because you are so beautiful to me." He grabbed her hair and held her into the next kiss. She could set his senses on fire with that tongue of hers. Loving a woman who reciprocated his love was a special gift. When she broke the kiss, he couldn't take his eyes off her. She centered his cock under her and arched her back as she lowered onto him. Forcing one hand to stay on her waist to steady her, the other slid up her ribs to her breasts and past to her beautiful throat. His hand curled around her neck and pulled her down for another kiss while he was inside her.

When she lifted and moved up and down, his eyes were glued to her. The way her body moved and swayed entranced him. He cupped her breasts and lightly teased her nipples. Her soft gasp and the stutter of the fluid motion of her hips told him how close she was. He sat up and rolled them. Her hair splayed out around her, a gorgeous dark halo on the white sheets. He lifted her leg and found a rhythm. She arched under him, drawing his eyes again. The woman was pure stimulation, sexy, beautiful, loving, caring—and his. He felt her tighten under him, and when she did, he lost himself inside her. The intensity of his orgasm popped red spots behind his eyelids.

He dropped his forehead to her shoulder. Her hands raked through his hair as he caught his breath. He lifted his head and stared at the woman who had taught him that love was a two-way street. She gave him more than he'd ever been able to give her. "I love you." He felt those words in the very fabric of his DNA. Amanda was his one true love. He'd had to wait for her, for her love, and that was the way destiny happened. Life didn't happen according to a schedule; it was messy, complicated, and surprising.

"I love you, too." She traced his eyebrows with her fingers before cupping his cheeks and pulling him down for another kiss.

# 18

Amanda stretched, luxuriating in the feel of the silky sheets against her body. She glanced over. The bed was empty, but that was normal. Frank was up with the sun. He'd probably already walked around the island two or three times. He was in perpetual motion, probably from a lifetime of hard work. His ranch was a beautiful thing. She'd loved visiting it when Jacob and Tori had Talon's christening there. The home he'd built for Elizabeth defied her ideas of a log home. Although, there was more of Frank in that house than Elizabeth.

She slid out of the bed and made her way to the shower. Every room had views of the ocean. The surf was a constant sound that became a backdrop for the serenity of the beautiful island. She had no idea how much staying on a private island cost. Anna told her not to worry about it, but she did. She'd saved and scrimped for her entire life. These lavish trips were something she'd always treasure, but this one would remain vivid in her mind forever.

Frank had asked her to marry him.

Lord, that had come as a shock. She'd just assumed they'd be lovers. Did she want more with Frank? Oh, Mary, Joseph, and the three wise men, yes! But she'd assumed he was happy with the arrangement they had. Arrangement? Time. Time was a better descriptor.

She washed her hair and conditioned it as she thought of the logistics of how a marriage would work. Frank had said he wanted her at the ranch. What did that mean for the home she had in Mississippi? There was little left of her memories of Chance, and that house was a big part of them. But Chance was gone; he wouldn't want her to hang onto the house. He was much more practical than that. Perhaps she'd offer it to the children. Lord knew they could afford it if they wanted it. But then again, it was just a house, and only Jason lived in Mississippi, and he lived on the coast.

The white, fluffy towel and the warm breeze off

the ocean dried her hair in no time. She put on a sundress and tied her hair up into a ponytail after applying sunscreen. It was another fabulous day. Glancing at the clock, she put a little pep in her step as she headed to the main area where they had their meals.

The vibe as soon as she walked in the door froze her to the floor. "What? What happened?" She looked between Gabriel and Frank.

"Tell her," Frank said and lifted his hand toward her. She walked across the floor and grabbed his hand.

"The children?"

Gabriel lifted a hand. "Everyone is okay. There was a situation involving Joseph. It's been fixed."

"What situation? What happened? I want details." Amanda's shoulders squared, and she leveled a stare at Gabriel. They'd worked together through the years to keep her children on the straight and narrow. She knew when he talked this way that the issues were usually dire.

She sank into a chair Frank pulled away from the table as Gabriel explained what Joseph had done. "It's all over the news. That's one of the reasons you're here."

Amanda drew a deep breath and let it out slowly.

"You knew this was happening, and you didn't tell me." She looked at Frank.

"I knew once we were on the island. I didn't tell you because there was nothing you could do. Worrying wasn't going to change anything."

"But it's resolved. You're sure?" She turned her attention to Gabriel.

"I am. Ember is in Atlanta now. She's heading to Aruba, and we need to go, too. Joseph has arranged for the entire family to fly down for the wedding."

"Wedding?" Amanda blinked and shot a look at Frank. "Whose wedding?"

Gabriel gave her an odd look. "Joseph and Ember's wedding. Why, whose wedding did you think I was talking about?"

Amanda turned to look at Frank. Her fiancé shrugged. "I didn't have a chance to tell him. He hit me with this news as soon as I came in this morning."

"Didn't tell me what?" Gabriel put his hands on his hips.

"Frank asked me to marry him last night. We were going to ask you to take us to the other island and for you and Anna to be our witnesses."

Frank's hand rested on her shoulder. "We can do that after we watch Joseph and Ember tie the knot."

She nodded. "I agree."

"Agree to what?" Anna walked in and stopped just as Amanda had. "What's going on?"

Gabriel filled her in, and Anna squealed, jumping up and down when he got to the part where Frank asked her to marry him. "We could have a double wedding!"

"No," both she and Frank spoke at the same time.

She laughed at Anna's crestfallen expression. "This is their day. We can get married here in the Bahamas after they have their ceremony."

Anna nodded. "You're right. So, we need to pack?"

"We do." Gabriel nodded. "I'll have the plane waiting. We'll take the boat back and fly to Aruba. Then we'll find a place for you two to get hitched."

"That sounds wonderful." Amanda nodded.

Anna grabbed her arm. "Tell me how he proposed."

Amanda glanced at Frank and smiled. "Under the stars, on the beach next to the surf, with the most wonderful words a woman could hear."

Frank strolled to the beach holding Amanda's hand. They were far enough from Joseph's home that the children wouldn't see them. Not that he cared, but he agreed with Amanda: this night was for celebration, for Joseph and Ember, and the joy of the King Family.

"I heard you tell Jacob that Clint was chasing after Keelee."

Frank grunted. "That's all Gerald. That man has steak taste on a hamburger budget, and he sees a match between Keelee and Clint as a way to grab what my family has spent generations building."

"Does she know what he's doing?"

"She's smart, but she's lonely, too." Frank shrugged. "Adam is doing better. He's talking well, and he's getting stronger, but he's stepped out of the way. Giving Clint a clear path while he avoids Keelee, so Clint doesn't have to work too hard."

Amanda sighed and stopped walking. She stared out into the ocean. "I wish I could help her. Being lonely isn't a reason to jump into a relationship." Amanda leaned into him. "I doubt Keelee would allow me to put in my two cents."

"Lord knows she needs to have some input. My sister-in-law Betty tries, but Keelee is headstrong."

"Betty! Frank, she's going to hate me moving in. It's her house."

Frank couldn't help the chuckle. "Are you kidding? She's been talking about moving to be with her son in the eastern side of the state. She's just waiting for an invite or a grandbaby. When one of those comes, she's gone. She's going to see you moving in as a respite. Stop looking for things to go wrong. This was meant to be."

Amanda's tense body relaxed against his. "You're right. I thought I'd sell the house in Mississippi after the first of the year."

That sure as hell didn't make sense. "Why?"

"Well, there's no sense in keeping it if I'm living in South Dakota."

Frank shook his head. "That house means things to your kids. Chance is part of that house. Keep it. We can travel down once or twice a year and make sure it's doing well. Hire someone to do the lawn and check on it. One day, one of your kids or grandkids is going to want to visit home. It needs to be there."

"Funny finding you out here." Joseph's voice from the darkness turned Frank. He and Ember walked hand and hand just as Frank and Amanda had.

"Not really," Frank rebutted. He extended his

hand. "Congratulations again. I'm very happy for both of you."

"Thank you." Ember's smile was dazzling even in the moonlight. "I just wish he hadn't put me through hell to reach this point."

Amanda shook her head. "I didn't know. I swear." Amanda shot a look at her son. "We'll talk about that later. I'm not going to fuss at you on your wedding day."

Joseph chuckled, "Thank you."

"You're welcome. What are you two doing for your honeymoon?" They all started walking back toward the house.

"We'll stay here. Then we'll head back to the annex if that's all right." Joseph looked over at Frank.

Frank nodded. "Plenty of room. Come back when you're ready."

"Thank you," Joseph said quietly. "It's going to be a transition for me."

"For both of us." Ember nodded.

"A good change." Amanda reached out and squeezed her son's arm.

"Will you be staying for a while?" Ember leaned forward to see Amanda as she asked.

"No, sweetie. We're going to leave in an hour or so with Gabriel and Anna. We have some things to tend to." Amanda squeezed his hand. "Besides, you don't want anyone hanging around on your honeymoon."

"That's for sure," Joseph growled.

Frank chuckled. "Amanda, may I suggest you make the rounds to your children and advise them of your imminent departure."

"I can do that," Amanda laughed.

"You don't have to—"

"Yes, she does," Joseph interrupted Ember.

Amanda shook her head. "Joseph, stop being a grump. Ember, don't take that attitude from him. You never used to let him get away with it."

"Oh, believe me, I have no plans on letting him be a grump."

Frank shook his head. Did that man know he'd traded the frying pan of his career for the fire of a feisty woman? Probably not. No doubt Joseph would relish the heat, though.

*Present Day, Marshall Ranch, South Dakota:*

"You were going to get married on our wedding day?" Ember sighed. "I'm so sorry!"

Joseph's head snapped around so he could see his wife. "Why?"

"It wasn't fair that they had to wait." Ember pushed her husband gently, but the man didn't move.

Frank grunted. "We got hitched."

"When? How? Where? You've never told anyone," Jared said. "Sorry, my investigative background is chiming in. Just the facts, only the facts." Jared deadpanned the last part.

A small wail came from the monitor on the table in front of Faith. "Don't stop. Jason, take notes. I'll be back down as soon as I get her fed and settled." Faith jumped up, grabbed the monitor, and ran out of the room and up the stairs.

Jade got up and stretched. "I need details. And a drink." She headed to the bar.

"You drink too much," Jewell shot at her sister.

"Yeah, not your place to judge, and I've always had a high tolerance," Jade snarked as she poured another small shot into her tumbler. "So, you got married in the Bahamas?"

"No, actually, New Orleans," Amanda admitted.

Jillian raised her hand and asked, "Why didn't you go back to the Bahamas?"

"That would be my fault," Gabriel admitted. "We

had an issue concerning a certain information extraction specialist that needed attention. I couldn't work that remotely."

Jason nodded. "That, I understand only too well." He pointed at Deacon and Ronan. "It isn't an easy job, but it's worth it."

"Charley gets to deal with that headache," Deacon snorted.

"Are you sure?" Gabriel lifted an eyebrow.

Ronan leaned forward. "I think the most important question to ask ourselves is, are we willing to give as much to the organization as the rest of you have? Walking in the footsteps of giants is a difficult task."

"You'll blaze your own path," Jacob said. "Don't try to be us. You bring your own unique assets to the organization. None of us would have imagined our lives to this point, and we're far from done. The uglier the world becomes, the more work there is to do."

Tori held up her hand. "I'm not letting this conversation move to business. Not yet anyway. I want to know why you got married in New Orleans without telling us about it."

# 19

*New Orleans, Louisiana, A day after Joseph's wedding:*

"Are you sure?" Gabriel asked Frank as they prepared to deplane from his private jet at Louis Armstrong International Airport.

"We can rent a car at the terminal. We're fine. Go take care of business." Frank extended his hand. "Thank you for everything. It was good to get away."

"But you're dying to be back at the ranch, aren't you?" Amanda moved up and took his hand.

"I'll admit it. If I stay away too long, I get itchy," Frank chuckled.

"Well, I, for one, am upset about not getting you two married." Anna pouted beside Gabriel.

"They can manage, I'm sure." Gabriel winked at Frank.

The hidden communication between them wasn't seen by either of the women, who were hugging each other goodbye. Frank gave Anna a quick hug and followed Amanda down the stairs. The private aviation company where they'd landed and taxied gave them a lift to the terminal, and Frank rented a full-size SUV. He was not an eco-friendly pedal car type of guy. Never would be.

"You missed the turn to the interstate." Amanda pointed at the exit to I-10 East.

"We aren't going home just yet."

"We aren't?" She turned to look at him. "Where are we going?"

"French Quarter." Frank smiled at her.

"Why?" She narrowed her eyes at him. "What did you do?"

"I can't tell you. It's a surprise." He chuckled at her huff of exasperation.

They pulled up to Jackson Square, and he put the vehicle into Park. "That's pretty." Amanda pointed to a white arch decorated in poinsettia flowers. It was a balmy sixty-seven degrees, and there were birds and children flitting about the park.

"Let's go look." He got out of the truck and came around to her side. He helped her out of the vehicle, and they made their way through the small park, past the bronze statue, to the far corner with the arch.

"Mr. Marshall?" A young man, maybe twenty-five years old, smiled and extended his hand.

"Mr. Randall?"

"Yes, sir. Are you ready? I have the witnesses." He motioned to a couple holding hands by the statue.

"Frank?" Amanda looked from the young man to the couple to the arch. "Are we getting married? Here?"

Frank lifted her hand and kissed the back of it. "I'm not waiting a minute longer."

Amanda's eyes misted up as she looked at him. "I love you."

He dropped a kiss onto her lips.

"Usually, the couples I marry wait until it's official before they kiss." Mr. Randall chuckled. "Miss Amanda, I'm Carlton Randall, a pastor here in this parish. It is my honor to marry you and Mr. Frank. Shall we?"

Frank stood beside his woman as the minister

said the words. It wasn't needed in his mind. He was already married to this woman in his heart, but the government had other ideas, and he wasn't going to leave any room for doubt should something happen to him.

"Do you have rings?"

"We don't." Frank turned and squeezed Amanda's hand. "My mother's ring is at home in the safe. I want you to have it."

Amanda smiled at him. "I didn't have time to look for a ring for you."

He placed his palm on her cheek. "I don't need anything to know I'm yours. Forever."

"Well, then, I can think of no better way to declare in the eyes of God and the State of Louisiana you are hereby married. You can kiss your bride."

Frank bent down to kiss her in front of God, the minister, and two witnesses he didn't know. They signed the license and were back in the truck five minutes later.

"I can't believe we just did that," Amanda laughed as they pulled onto the interstate.

"About time," Frank grunted, which made her laugh more.

"So, when are we going to tell the kids?"

"We'll figure it out." He wasn't worried about

telling them. "But not today, maybe not tomorrow. We're on our honeymoon."

Amanda's mouth opened. "Honeymoon? Frank, I don't have any clothes. I'm wearing the one good dress I have that's clean."

"You won't need clothes for a day or two." He looked at her and watched her blush. "We'll have the laundry service at the hotel take care of that for you."

"Where are we staying?"

"The Omni." He pointed in the direction of the hotel they'd stayed at on one of his quick trips down from South Dakota.

"I love the Omni. The old-world charm and rich colors and the staff are so nice." She took his hand. "You spoil me."

"You deserve to be spoiled." He lifted her hand and kissed the back of it.

Frank handed the rental key over to the valet. They strolled through the lobby. The white marble tile was buffed to a high polish. He liked this hotel, too. It wasn't one of those modern monstrosities. The interior didn't jar his sensibilities. The lush greenery blended with the opulence of the structure. They checked in and walked up the stairs to the suite he'd reserved.

"Oh, Frank!" Amanda spun in the living area. "This is too much. It's too expensive." She gasped at the two-person jetted tub tucked off the bathroom. "You didn't need to do this."

He grunted at her. Yes, he did. He'd give her the queen's crown jewels if he thought for an instant she'd benefit from having them. Hell, he had plenty of money. More money than he knew what to do with, actually. In part because he owned ten percent of Guardian Security but also because of how he'd managed the ranch through the years.

She came up to him and hugged him from behind. "I will never take you or the way you treat me for granted. I promise you that I cherish everything you do for me."

He turned and wrapped his arms around her. "It's been a long time since you've had someone to watch out for you."

"No, that's not true. The children always check in on me."

He grunted again, and they began to sway to music he was sure no one else could hear. "It's not the same. Having someone who loves you, who is with you every day to protect you, to care for you, and to spoil you."

She sighed into him. "You're right. It's not the same thing."

He took his time making love to her. There was no rush, the sounds of New Orleans didn't penetrate the room, and even if they had, neither would have noticed.

When she lay in his arms, soft and relaxed after they'd made love, she asked, "You want me to have your mom's ring?"

He nodded, knowing his chin moved her hair, and she could feel the action. "Ma forbade me from giving it to Elizabeth. Made me promise her."

Amanda elbowed up. "What?"

"They didn't get along. My ma tolerated her and loved the girls. Elizabeth and Ma tried, but the two women couldn't see eye to eye on anything. When Ma died, I think it alleviated a pressure on Elizabeth. She didn't say so, but ..."

Amanda rested her chin on his chest. "You didn't have a good marriage?"

Frank sighed. "I've never said this to another soul, but no. I tried like hell, but after she got pregnant with Tori, she moved to another bedroom. We lived in the same house, but we were friends who were raising children. I'll never speak ill of her to the girls or anyone else. She and I were dealt a bad hand, and we played it out. Neither of us won in that game. Elizabeth especially. She was a good woman."

Amanda nodded. "Chance and I married against his mother's wishes. There was a horrible scene. It broke him to leave his family, but he did. For me." She moved, sitting up beside him. Her hair fell over her shoulders.

He grabbed some of it and let it fall through his fingers. "Why didn't she want him to marry you?"

Amanda shrugged. "I grew up in a small town in Mississippi. Chance and I met in a bar when I went to the East Coast. I went to Washington D.C. as a graduation present. My grandma and grandpa had saved for years. I was eighteen and looked older. They didn't card me at the bar." Frank could have made a quip about her being a naughty girl, but he could see this story was hard for her to tell, so he kept his words to himself. "I only had soda." She looked up at him. "I know that's hard to believe, but I didn't want to get into trouble. So I'm sitting in there watching all the people. The clothes, Frank. Business suits and dresses that cost more than my bus fare to D.C., let me tell you." She chuckled. "I had like three dresses that were very basic. I was wearing one. Chance noticed me right away. He came over, and we started talking. I told him right away that I was only in D.C. for the weekend. It didn't seem to matter to him. He was bigger than life and handsome. He walked me back to my hotel that night and was there the next morning to pick me up for breakfast. He took me around D.C. and showed me everything. There was an instant connection between us. I felt it, so did he. But we didn't act on it. I got on the bus and headed back to Mississippi. Chance followed me. He met my mom and dad. He got a job in New Orleans working for one of the prestigious law firms. There were eight or ten names before 'Law Firm' if you know what I mean."

He chuffed. "Yup. Know exactly what you mean."

She nodded. "We fell in love, he asked me to marry him, and he took me home to meet his parents. Frank, I was a hick, and I was also a virgin. We'd never gone past a certain point. I was going to wear white at my wedding. No questions asked." She sighed and flicked her hair over her shoulder. "His mother reacted badly to his news and to me. She called me some really awful things, accused me of gold-digging and of being a tramp. She forbade Chance to marry me. That went over like a lead balloon."

"Chance knew what a beautiful person you

were." Frank knew, too. Any person who had eyes could see the kindness and gentleness in her.

"He left with me, and we went back to Mississippi. In the meantime, his mother, who was very powerful, made moves, too. Chance was let go from his job in New Orleans, and no law firm in the state would even talk to him about a job. He found a deputy sheriff's job open and took it. We got married and lived off my pay and his. Until we started having children. My mom and dad babysat for the first couple, but as you know, we had a big family." She laughed. "I worked when Chance wasn't, so at least one of us was home with the kids. It was hard and messy and the most wonderful time." She smiled at him. "Then he was murdered." She shook her head and looked away. "I was so broken. So were the children. I forced myself to be there for them and to mend myself. If Gabriel hadn't contacted me about that life insurance policy, I don't know what we would have done."

"You would have survived," he supplied for her.

"Yeah. We would have." She smiled at him. "I had a good marriage, Frank. I loved Chance. I wanted you to know that even though I had that ... this, what is between us, is a totally different type of love. My love for you isn't a comparison to my love for Chance. It is its own entity. I can't compare them, I won't, but I know that I love you as deeply and as much as I ever loved him. I will love you until my last breath, and I thank God I have you."

Frank stared at her for a moment. "I've never had what you've had. But I know what you mean. I'll never compare what we share to what Elizabeth and I had. It wouldn't be fair to our departed, and it wouldn't be fair to each other. Our life, Amanda, is a new journey."

She leaned down and kissed him. "Thank you for understanding what I was trying to say."

Frank deepened the kiss and threaded his fingers through her fall of thick black hair. When he released her, he whispered, "Love has a way of making everything clearer."

Amanda straddled him and bent down, her full, soft breasts pressed into his chest. "These people who say you don't talk much don't know you very well, do they? You say the most beautiful things." He rolled his eyes, and she laughed. "I've got your number, Frank Marshall. You are a big softie."

"No one will believe it." He moved, rolling them over so he was on top of her.

She laughed as she flopped onto the mattress. "Now, show me how much you love me."

## 20

*Present Day, Marshall Ranch, South Dakota:*

"That's where you were when you found out about Keelee? New Orleans?" Tori asked.

Amanda nodded. "Thanks to Jacob tracking us down. Neither Frank nor I had our cell phones charged."

"Well, I didn't track you down; Jewell did."

"Yeah, we didn't know you two were together." Jewell grabbed a handful of mixed nuts from the dish on the tray in front of her. "I was looking for Frank."

Tori shot a look at her husband. "Why didn't you tell me that you found my dad in New Orleans?"

Jacob blinked and shrugged. "I ... ahh ..."

"I answered the phone, Tori. I think Jacob was being tactful in forgetting that detail." Amanda chuckled as Jacob's face turned red.

Tori stared at her husband, then smiled. "You thought what? That our parents were just shacking up?"

"What's wrong with that?" Jade asked. Everyone turned to look at her. She threw up her hands. "Consenting adults. Am I the only one who remembers this detail?"

"I didn't want to make any assumptions, and with you so stressed about Keelee and being pregnant, I erred on the side of caution." He shifted uncomfortably in his seat.

Tori leaned over and kissed him. "Thank you."

He smiled at her and dropped his arm over her shoulders. "Then it took forever to get them to South Dakota."

Frank groaned. "Which reminds me, I never bought that private plane."

. . .

# Frank

*Louis Armstrong International Airport, New Orleans, Louisiana, three days after Joseph's wedding:*

Amanda put her hand on Frank's leg. If he tapped his heel any harder, there would be a hole in the floor at the gate where they were sitting. "Breathe," she whispered.

The plane they were supposed to take to Dallas was late because of weather. It was a rotator that flew back and forth between the two cities. They had a limited window to make it to Dallas and get the flight to Rapid City, a flight that only happened once a day.

"Maybe you should call Betty and see if she's heard anything." They'd pulled their cell phones out of the luggage and charged them while they were packing and getting flights lined up.

"I called her a half hour ago, and she said she'd call if she heard anything," Frank grumped. "I'm going to buy a plane."

Amanda blinked. "A plane?"

"Won't need to wait on others that way." Frank's heel started tapping out a staccato beat against the floor again.

"Adam went after her, and Betty said he found

her. He'll take care of her. You know he worked with Jacob, and you know he's capable. He's a doctor." She repeated all the things she'd been telling herself to keep from freaking out. Not that it worked because her stomach was tied in knots. Between her children and his, something was always happening.

"It was below zero. People don't last in that type of weather. What was she thinking? I've taught her better." Frank leaned his elbows on his thighs and clasped his hands together.

"Frank, she learned how to survive from you. She's smart. She knew to seek shelter, and Adam found her. She went up there because Clint told her there was a family who was in need. She's just like you. She'll do anything she can to help someone out. That was what she was thinking. Being mad at her isn't going to do anything in this situation."

He drew a deep breath and rolled his head so he could see her. "Please stop making sense. You're ruining my righteous indignation."

Amanda smiled and laughed. Frank sat up and put his arm around her. "Thank you." He kissed the top of her head. They listened to the gate agent announce the arrival of their plane.

Of course, they missed the plane to Rapid City. "We can get you into Denver. Another airline has a flight from Denver to Rapid in the morning, and it would get you there four hours before our flight." The gate attendant looked up from her computer.

"Book it." Frank ground the words out and slid a black credit card across the desk.

"Thank you," Amanda added with a polite smile. Frank grunted, and Amanda suppressed another smile. They walked down to the gate where they would board the next plane. "I'm buying a plane. Hiring a pilot to be on call just like Gabriel. I have the money."

"Are you ranting?" She squeezed his hand.

"I'm not ranting; I'm plotting." He gave a quick nod as if to agree with himself.

"Oh, good to know," Amanda said as they found two seats together. "Call Betty and tell her about the schedule change."

∼

"You're here! Hi, Amanda." Betty opened the door for them. "Adam brought her home. She's okay. Well, she's not, but she will be. They're upstairs. Wait, Frank, I need to tell you about Clint."

Frank stopped and dropped their suitcases. He

was tired, and he wanted to see his daughter and make sure she was okay. "What about him?"

"Ah, he showed up at the line cabin and attacked Keelee. Beat her up real good."

"What?" Amanda gasped. "Where was Adam?"

"He was retrieving the other snowmobile. She has a bad concussion. She's already talked to the sheriff. Lord, that wasn't a good thing. The sheriff made insinuations about Adam and Keelee."

Frank felt the hair on the back of his neck lift. "What?"

"It was horrible, but Jason and the twins kept Adam from doing something stupid." Betty grabbed his arm. "Adam went after her and found her. He and Jason tried to track down Clint, but the boy flew the coop."

Dixon and Drake appeared at the top of the stairs. He pointed to the luggage. "Take this up for me?"

"You got it" and "On it" were said in unison as they started down the stairs.

Frank nodded. He'd process all of this later. Right then, he needed to see Keelee and make sure she was okay. He started up the stairs when the twins hit the ground floor. Amanda shouted after him, "Remember, Adam found her, and she's going to be okay."

He grunted at his wife's wise words. He was pissed. What the hell had happened? He'd find Clint and teach that boy what happened when someone messed with his daughters.

His long legs ate up the distance to his daughter's room. He opened the door and walked halfway into her bedroom before he heard their voices.

"Your doctor hasn't cleared you to resume normal activities. Let Dixon and Drake take care of it today. Besides, Dr. Wheeler is on his way here. I'd like you to talk with him about the assault." That was Adam's voice. Why was he in the bathroom with Keelee? Was he changing bandages? Frank took another step forward.

"I appreciate your concern, but I don't need to talk about it. It happened. It's over. I'm not worried about him coming around here to carry through with his threat."

Frank stopped still. *What threat? What in the hell ...*

Keelee continued, "He won't come anywhere near this place. He's not stupid. Crazy ... okay, I'll give you that, but he's definitely not an idiot."

"Really? He's not an idiot? He lost enough mental capacity to assault you. That makes him crazy *and* an idiot." Frank took another step. Adam was right. "I guess your mind was occupied with other things. Otherwise, you'd realize how silly that comment was."

Frank saw Adam first. Half-naked. Make that three-quarters naked. His mind spun out of control when he heard his daughter laugh, "Hey! I have enough bruising on my face. I don't need to run into a wall of solid muscle, too!" He crossed his arms and leveled a glare at his daughter and her ... lover. Keelee hid behind Adam once she noticed Frank and tried to smile as she asked, "Oh ... hi, Daddy ... ahh ... When did you get home?"

He blanked. Truly and honestly, his mind went blank. Never in his wildest dreams ... Keelee and Doc? What threat? He flexed and released his fists and jaw, trying everything he knew to put one logical foot in front of the other. Finally, his mouth caught up with his brain. "Girl, get your ass into some clothes." He cast Adam an icy glare because there was so much to say, to question, and to demand, and yet he couldn't put those words together in any manner. Adam straightened and held his ground as Keelee slid farther behind him, hiding even more from his glare. Frank pointed to Adam and ground out, "You. Downstairs. Now."

He turned and made his way out of the bedroom and straight to his office.

"Did you ... Hey, what's wrong?" Amanda ran after him as he made a beeline to his office. She shut the door behind them. "Frank, is Keelee okay?" She set a cup of coffee on the desk. "This is for you."

"Thank you. She's fine, I'd say. Caught her and Adam coming out of the bathroom damn near naked. Obvious what had been taking place." He put his hands on his hips and stared at the snow covering the ground in front of his office window.

Amanda chuckled and sat down on his desk. Her legs swung as she spoke. "She's alive, she's safe, and she's in love. Jared called just a moment ago and said Adam has his memory back. That's a good thing."

She was right; of course, she was. "I overheard something about Clint issuing a threat to her. Her face is messed up. He hurt her."

Amanda was up and by his side in a minute. "Find out what needs to be done. Then we'll have breakfast and coffee. I'll go whip up something. I love you, and you need to ask questions about what happened here. Don't put that young man on the offensive. He loves her." Frank grunted again, and

Amanda toed up and kissed his cheek. "I'm going to the kitchen."

He nodded and watched her walk away.

A knock at the door sounded a second before Amanda reached to open it. Adam stood on the other side of it. "Miss Amanda?"

Amanda pulled Adam into a hug. "Oh, my sweet boy, Jared told me you regained your memory. I'm so happy for you."

Adam hugged her and then pulled away. "I have. I'm sorry I didn't stick around in Aruba, but I had to get back. I had to see Keelee."

Amanda cupped his cheek with her hand and nodded. "I know, sweetie, and from all accounts, it's a damn good thing you came back when you did."

A snort from Frank drew their attention. Amanda chuckled and patted Adam on the arm. "He's really just an old softie. Where's Keelee?"

Adam's expression told him he didn't agree with Amanda's description. Good, he could work with that. Adam answered, "She's going to meet me in the kitchen. We slept in and missed breakfast."

Frank muttered, "No shit." He didn't cotton to swearing, but it seemed this morning things were out of the norm anyway.

"Oh, Adam, son, you really need to talk with

Frank. I'll make us some breakfast and make sure there's more than enough for you and Keelee." She pushed Adam into the room as she spoke. "Now go. Talk. I'll keep Keelee company." The door shut quietly behind her.

Adam turned and met his stare. Then the man did the one thing that would light his tinder.

He laughed.

"You find something amusing here, son?"

"Ah, actually, yes, sir, I do," Adam admitted

He failed to see the humor in any of this. Adam would have to explain in detail what he found so damn humorous. "And what exactly do you find so funny?"

"That two consenting adults who happen to love each other got caught in a compromising situation. Honestly, I feel like I'm a fourteen-year-old juvenile delinquent, not a thirty-five-year-old adult and an established doctor. With a great career, I might add."

Frank grunted and rubbed the stubble on his chin. Well, there was that. He was bone-tired and worried to the end of his frayed nerves. He scratched his chin again. He needed a shave. Frank motioned toward two large leather chairs. "Sit down, son. We need to have a talk."

Frank grabbed his coffee mug off the desk and sat opposite Adam.

He took a sip of his coffee and gathered his thoughts. Amanda was right; he didn't want to put the boy on the offensive. Not yet anyway. "Tell me what happened on the mountain. From the beginning."

"I got here about five. Betty was fit to be tied. Keelee had taken a snowmobile up to an old homestead because Clint told her he'd seen a family up there. Blizzard hit while she was out."

"Was there a family up there?" Frank leaned forward on his forearms, waiting for a reply.

"No, sir. I did a search of the house when I was looking for her. Nobody had been in that place in eons."

Frank nodded and waited expectantly, and Adam continued, "I found her. She'd fallen through the roof of an old root cellar. The plunge banged her up a bit. She'd hit her head, twisted her ankle, and was damn near frozen, but she had a small fire and was protected from the wind. She could have survived a while longer if I hadn't gone and found her."

He'd been up to that old homestead. That fall had to have been at least ten or twenty feet. With the snow falling, it wouldn't be dry. Even though the wind would have been blocked a bit, the temperatures were still subzero. He leveled a stare at Adam. "That the truth?"

Adam pushed a hand through his hair and admitted, "Hell, you know, sir—probably not. It was too damn cold. She'd have suffered severe hypothermia, probably fallen asleep, and died before morning." Adam rolled his shoulders. "But I got to her, got her back to the line shack, and took care of her."

"When did Koehler show?"

"Sometime the next day. The next morning, I left her alone at the line shack, returned to the homestead, and retrieved her snowmobile." He stared straight at Frank and swore, "I would have never left her if I had any indication Clint was going to show up or that he would hurt her. I had no idea he was violent or disturbed."

Frank grunted. "Disturbed. Fancy way to say the boy finally lost it. That fucking father of his pushed the boy over the deep end. Gerald's pure poison. I keep those boys working here to try to protect them." He wished he could just buy Gerald out, but that old codger was pure mean, and honestly, Frank didn't want anything to do with the bastard. *Shit.* He snapped his head up and pegged Adam with a stare. "Christian okay?"

Adam nodded and leaned forward in his chair again. "Jason and I brought him here. We'll set him up at a good college and pay his way as long as he gets good grades and is a responsible citizen. We've agreed to split his costs. We'll explain that to him. We're wrapping it up as a Christmas gift. It'll make it harder for him to refuse. But you need to know the real reason why he's here."

Frank narrowed his eyes. What the hell had Gerald done now? "Yeah? And why is that?"

Adam sighed, "I'm making assumptions, and for that matter, so is Jason, but we think there's more at play than the boy is letting on. He's terrified, and if I were a betting man, I'd say he's afraid because he's ... Well, I think he's been abused by his family because he's gay. Is that going to be a problem?"

Frank didn't understand the question. What the hell did the boy's sexual orientation have to do with anything? "Why the hell would it be? Son, I got no right to cast any stones. I know that boy. He's the gentle kind. Christian wouldn't hurt a thing unless he was forced into it, and that asshole Gerald forced him into it ... regularly." Frank turned his attention from Adam to the window. "If I could've moved those boys here, I would have. Can't help but think I didn't do enough." He sighed and glanced back at Adam. "What about Gregg? He here, too?"

Adam quirked his eyebrow up. "Who's Gregg?"

Frank snorted. "The middle brother. I'll take a trip to the Koehlers' today. Offer Gregg a full-time position here."

"Frank, there's more. Christian was beaten by his brothers or his father. He's not saying which, but someone took out some serious aggression on that boy. Broke his arm. I was worried about his zygomatic bone, but it wasn't compromised."

Frank blinked. What did Adam say? In English, maybe? "His zygo-what?"

"Zygomatic bone—cheekbone. From what Christian said, Clint's gone. Guardian is watching for him, and Jared is working with the state police and the local law enforcement officers to ensure all the bases are covered. Clint dumped his truck in Rapid City, but there's no trace of him."

"Holy hell. The first time I spend more than a long weekend away from the ranch in two years, and all this shit breaks loose." Frank rubbed his face with both hands and fell back into the plush leather chair. "All right, now that I got a handle on that, I need some answers. First, is Keelee all right physically? Those bruises are the extent of her injuries, right?"

Adam nodded. "She also sustained a concussion, but she's going to be fine."

Frank released a long breath and nodded. "Second, Christian is safe, and you'll make sure he stays out of Gerald's reach. Just so Gerald doesn't get any ideas, make sure Christian stays in the ranch house, not in the bunkhouse. Understood?"

"Yeah, the Wonder Twins hooked him up with a room down the hall from them."

Frank closed his eyes and nodded. "I'll take care of Gregg, but I need to get one other matter settled first." Drawing a lungful of air, he let it out, sounding a little bit like a pressure cooker that was about to explode, which, quite frankly, he was. "Son, what exactly are your intentions toward my daughter?"

Adam gulped and swallowed, but he didn't hesitate to respond, which said a lot about the man. "I love her. I'm going to marry her if you give me your blessings." Adam ran his hands through his hair again and stood up. "I don't know who in the hell I'm trying to fool. I'm marrying her even if you don't give your blessings. Life has taken two years from us. I'll be damned if I wait much longer to make her my wife."

He fought a smile. The man would do; he really would. It was a good match. "That so?" he grunted.

Adam nodded and spoke clearly, "Yes."

Frank cocked his head. Keelee was her own woman. It wouldn't matter what he said if she wasn't on board with the idea of matrimony, Adam was sunk. He asked, "What did she say about that? Can't imagine she'd let you run that show."

Adam smiled. "Haven't asked her yet. I wanted to do this right. I wanted to ask you, but as I said …"

Frank lifted a hand, "Yeah, son, I got it. And you got it. My blessing, that is. When you plan on asking her?" Frank stood and stretched.

Adam stood, too. "Christmas Eve. Figured a ring would be my present to her. Which I still need to buy. Crap, I need to get Jason to fly me someplace with a decent jeweler. I don't even know her ring size. How the hell do I find that out?" Adam's face flushed, and his eyes searched the room, landing on nothing in particular.

Frank looked at the picture on the wall of Keelee's mother. "Huh. Well, if you're open to a suggestion, maybe you could get her mom's engagement ring reset. Kind of sentimental and such. Put your own stones with it. Make it yours but give her a piece of her mom, too. Her mom's ring fits her hand. Seen her admiring it one day. Size six."

Adam smiled and nodded. "I'd be honored, sir. Thank you."

Frank watched the man move toward the door before he spoke, "Oh, and Adam?"

Adam stopped and turned to meet his gaze. "Sir?"

He said the words from the bottom of his heart, meaning every syllable, "In case there was any doubt, if you hurt that girl again, there won't be a place you can hide from me. You got that, boy?"

Adam swallowed hard but nodded. "I love her, sir. I admit I've screwed up. If I hadn't lost my memory, I would have been back here the day after the mission, begging her to forgive me and asking for a second chance. We took the long way to this point, but there isn't a force on this earth that will separate us again."

Frank grunted and slapped Adam on the shoulder. "Glad we had this little talk, son. Now, how about we both get some food?"

Adam grinned. "Yes, sir."

Frank grabbed his coffee cup and said, "Just one more thing ... Son, lock the damn door from now on."

"Ahh ... yes, sir." Frank could hear the embarrassment in the man's voice. He wouldn't lie; he got satisfaction out of it.

∽

Present Day, *Marshall Ranch, South Dakota:*

"But you didn't let anyone know you were married for weeks!" Jillian threw her hands up. "Why?"

"Because of them." Frank nodded at Keelee and Adam. "It was a time for them and the family. We were going to wait until the New Year to tell everyone, but I sat beside that Christmas tree and watched each one of the people I cared about more than anything in the world and figured it was time."

Faith jogged down the stairs. "How much did I miss? Your little princess thought it was morning." She sat down beside Jason.

"I'll fill you in." Jason dropped his arm over her shoulder.

"I missed everything?" She looked from person to person.

"Yup. Your timing sucks." Jade quipped.

"So not fair." Faith swung around. "Tomorrow morning. Coffee ladies, I want to hear everything."

"Nope. Sorry, tomorrow morning we have a staff meeting in the new CCS." Gabriel stood and extended his hand to Anna. "We'll say good night."

Anna shook her head. "I should help with the dishes and trays."

"I've got it." Jillian jumped up.

"Me, too." Taty stood, and so did Jewell and Jade.

"I'll help, but you're going to fill me in." Faith demanded as she got up.

"I'll go supervise." Amanda kissed him on the cheek and followed the women folk into the kitchen.

"What's the staff meeting about?" Deacon asked.

"You'll find out tomorrow." Gabriel looked at Tori and winked.

Frank didn't miss the communication between the two. He leveled a stare at his daughter as the others started to leave. "I'll be up in a minute," Tori said to Jacob before moving to sit beside Frank. "I'm okay. I talked to Doc Wheeler today. He thinks I'm finally processing the emotions of the event after all these months. It's not easy, but I know with Jacob by my side, I can get there."

Thank God. They'd all been worried about her, about her not facing what had happened. "Good. What's going on between you and Gabriel?"

"Something I think will help me and Jacob, in a

roundabout way, and the organization as a whole." She kissed him on the cheek as Amanda had. "You found a diamond when you found Amanda, Dad. I'm so happy for both of you. I know I've told you that in the past, but she is your soulmate. I've found mine, so I know what type of love that is."

He watched his daughter walk up the stairs and breathed a sigh of relief until he remembered that she and Gabriel had a surprise staff meeting. Knowing his old friend and his daughter, something big was about to happen.

He heard Amanda walking behind him. Her hand on his shoulder was warm and loving. He relished the moments they were together. "It wasn't so bad, was it?"

He smiled and shook his head. "Any time I spend thinking of us and our life together is good. Real good."

"You say the sweetest things, Frank." Amanda kissed his cheek. He chuckled. "Don't always say them."

Amanda chuckled. "That's okay, honey. I speak fluent grunt."

## 21

Jason sat at the head of the table. At his right was Gabriel and then Frank next to him. His brothers Joseph, Jared, Jacob, then Tori, Jewell, Zane, Dixon, Joy, Drake, Jillian, Mike, Taty, Adam, Ronan, Deacon, and Kaeden Lang, the current handler for the Shadows, comprised the rest of the table. A full house, to say the least.

Jason cleared his throat and brought all the scattered conversations to a halt. "Today is the first day of the new Guardian Security. Jewell, slide one, please."

The slide he asked for popped onto the screen at the end of the room. All heads turned toward the current organizational chart. "This is how Guardian used to be structured. You'll all notice the HR, IT, and Operator functions running from my position down. Domestic Operations, Overseas Operations, and Shadow Operations also fell from my position and were routed through the various heads of the department. This was acceptable due to the co-located facility.

"Jewell, please move on to slide number two." Jason waited for the slide to change. "Lessons learned from the siege on the D.C. location and the ranch. First and foremost, we are vulnerable even if we don't believe we are. All moves forward will acknowledge this fact in all situations. Linear direction and responsibility did work, but if all of us were taken out, the organization would have ceased to function because there would have been no one to take charge. The Rose was the only entity not compromised because no one knows its location." Heads around the table nodded up and down. "We need to transform in order to eradicate the vulnerabilities we were operating under. Next slide."

Gabriel spoke. "Jason and I have discussed at length the new composition of Guardian. Domestic Operations will work independently of the other sections. We will supply trained computer technicians to process the work you require done: traces, backgrounds, monitoring, etc. Jewell and Zane have developed a mandatory skill-set training for people working with your portion of the organization."

Jared leaned forward. "Independent?"

"As in no visible connection to the other portions of Guardian. As far as anyone knows, the company has fractured. Domestic Operations will be the only portion of the business visible to the public," Jason clarified.

"But we're not going to be all that's left of Guardian, right?" Jade looked down the table at Jason and Gabriel.

"Guardian will always fall under one umbrella. However, the appearance of divesting the overseas operations from Domestic Operations limits the liabilities to Dom Ops," Gabriel stated in no uncertain terms.

"What about Overseas Operations?" Jacob leaned forward.

"That, we will wait on for a moment." Gabriel nodded to Jewell, and another slide appeared. "The Rose will continue training. However, the Thorn Team concepts are on hold. Joseph, you'll take over Shadow training at the Rose. Lycos will report to you, and you will be in charge of all the Shadows."

Jacob leaned forward. "Excuse me?"

Gabriel held up a hand. "Jewell?"

Another slide lit up the screen. "Overseas Operations will be split into two parts. The teams and missions that you run, Jacob, will go on as normal. You will run operations out of our new headquarters in Colorado."

"No." Jacob shook his head. "We aren't leaving the Rose."

Tori put her hand on his arm. "Listen to the rest." She smiled at him, and he narrowed his eyes at her before swinging his attention back to Gabriel.

Gabriel tipped his head in Jewell's direction. Another slide popped up, showing Overseas Operations split into two columns. "When our facilities in Colorado are ready, The GHoST Element will be headed up by Tori. She will oversee the development of the element, and if it goes as we expect, it will expand into its own section with Guardian Security. Until that point, Tori and Jacob will share headquarter space and run all operations in tandem, ensuring our new Ghost Element, as we are calling it, has the training needed. Specifically, hostage negotiation, hostage rescue tactics, special weapons and tactics, linguistics, and rapid deployment methodologies. These teams will deploy around the world, but their primary focus will be here in the United States."

Kaeden Lang cocked his head. "Is there a need? Don't cities have their own hostage negotiation and response teams?"

"Cities do, but they're chronically underfunded. In order to respond, we would be requested by the jurisdiction in charge of the incident. We will work in conjunction with the FBI's task forces should they be fielded," Tori answered.

"As you know, both Faith and Tori were abducted and transported out of the area where they were taken. The local authorities did not have the ability to track or locate them. Jewell did, even in her limited capacity at the time. We can go anywhere in the United States as we are federally recognized," Jason added.

Drake spun in his chair. "What about the ranch?"

Mike nodded his head in agreement. "The ranch will remain a rehab and training hub for Domestic Operations. We're incorporating a more robust early warning system around the perimeter, and all management and hospital facilities will go underground. The only buildings top side will be classrooms and support facilities."

"CCS?" Joseph asked.

"CCS and the Operators will be hidden as the Rose and the Colorado facility. They will work out of nodes, coverage will be redundant, and all backups will dump into a mainframe we are going to install into the Rose's facility. Communications at the Rose will be upgraded, and there will be five Operators assigned to the Rose, five to the new Colorado facility, and the remaining twenty will work from remote nodes around the world with the best encryption, masking, and shielding available to mankind." Gabriel leaned forward and put his elbows on the conference table. "Anubis will work for Joseph and still run day-to-day operations for the Shadows from here. Zane will stay his backup. CCS Operators will work here at the ranch, at the Rose, and at the Colorado facility when it is done. Nodes, such as the one Jewell and Zane will run, will be strategically placed to ensure security, the same as we will provide for the Operators."

"HR for us?" Jacob popped the question.

"We're hiring Rio North to take on the HR arm of the operation. Shadows and other specialized operatives will continue as is. They don't exist. Pay and any benefits will be handled by myself, Jason, or our appointed representatives only."

Joseph leaned forward. "So, no real organizational change except for adding an element and hiding our resources so no one will be able to find us again."

Gabriel nodded. "The Thorn Teams are on hold. People will be assigned to either Jared or Jacob's section or back to you in Shadow land."

Anubis sighed. "We have a few people in limbo status."

Joseph nodded. "We do."

"Frank and I are working on a plan for those people," Gabriel answered.

"Frank?" There were several who said his name at the same time.

Gabriel nodded. "He's been a silent partner, sounding board, and advisor for some time now."

Mike spoke, and everyone looked his way. "Before the attack, Asp was talking about starting a sniper school up here at the Annex. With the addition of the GHoST Element, that school would be a good thing. He and Billy are willing to tag-team to start that program."

Gabriel looked at Jason. Jason nodded. "I remember you mentioned something about that after I was discharged. Sorry, it fell by the side. I don't have a problem with the school. I need to see a concept and the training plan. Have them start working on it."

"Done." Mike nodded.

"Deacon and Ronan will start working with the organization in the new year. Charley will work under Jason to assist him and learn the ropes. Dan will be available to you, Kaeden, and Joseph to help with the Baby Shadows. He has a way with them."

"That he does," Joseph snorted. "Thankful for it, too."

"Amen," Kaeden echoed.

"Any other questions?" There was silence around the table. "This is the future, ladies and gentlemen. Let's embrace it." Jason held up a hand as everyone started to stand. "Jacob and Tori, if you could stay for a moment."

The rest of the people found their way out, and when the door shut, Jason turned to Jacob. "Tori came to us and asked if she could set up the unit."

Jacob nodded and glanced at his wife. "I'm concerned it will be too much for you."

"Which is why the Shadows are solely with Joseph now. You won't have any distractions or hooks into your time. You can run both the element and the Overseas Operations if things get too much for Tori." Gabriel looked from Jacob to Frank.

"But they won't. I may need breathers, but Jacob, I need to have something to work toward. I need to have something to pull me out of this pit. I want to make a difference to other people who are experiencing what I have. Will I be better overnight? No, but this gives me the opportunity to take things a step at a time. There is a lot to do before we'll be ready."

Jacob cupped his palm over her cheek. "I have you, babe. Whatever it takes."

She smiled and toed up to kiss him. "I know you do, and I know you'll be here as long as it takes."

"We're good?" Jason asked from the head of the table.

Jacob glanced back at him. "Never better."

"Then we're done here." Jason, Jacob, and Tori left the room. Frank leaned back in his chair. "Well, that went well."

Gabriel nodded. "We're making strides. It was a tough go for a while, but we'll get there."

"A new dawn for the greatest security agency in the free world." Frank glanced at the table and remembered the faces of his family, if not by blood, then by brotherhood.

"I once told you that the people who sat around this table were the tip of the spear. I was wrong. They're the entire weapon. Guardian is only as good as her people, and she is home to the best."

Frank nodded and stood. He extended his hand to his life-long friend. "To many, many more years of being the weapon that brings peace and security to our world."

"For as long as it takes." Gabriel shook his hand. "For as long as it takes."

CLICK HERE to enjoy the next stories in the Guardian World!

Zeke, Hollister, Book 2

Valkyrie, Guardian Shadow World, Book 9

## ALSO BY KRIS MICHAELS

**Kings of the Guardian Series**

Jacob: Kings of the Guardian Book 1

Joseph: Kings of the Guardian Book 2

Adam: Kings of the Guardian Book 3

Jason: Kings of the Guardian Book 4

Jared: Kings of the Guardian Book 5

Jasmine: Kings of the Guardian Book 6

Chief: The Kings of Guardian Book 7

Jewell: Kings of the Guardian Book 8

Jade: Kings of the Guardian Book 9

Justin: Kings of the Guardian Book 10

Christmas with the Kings

Drake: Kings of the Guardian Book 11

Dixon: Kings of the Guardian Book 12

Passages: The Kings of Guardian Book 13

Promises: The Kings of Guardian Book 14

The Siege: Book One, The Kings of Guardian Book 15

The Siege: Book Two, The Kings of Guardian Book 16

A Backwater Blessing: A Kings of Guardian Crossover Novella

Montana Guardian: A Kings of Guardian Novella

**Guardian Defenders Series**

Gabriel

Maliki

John

Jeremiah

Frank

**Guardian Security Shadow World**

Anubis (Guardian Shadow World Book 1)

Asp (Guardian Shadow World Book 2)

Lycos (Guardian Shadow World Book 3)

Thanatos (Guardian Shadow World Book 4)

Tempest (Guardian Shadow World Book 5)

Smoke (Guardian Shadow World Book 6)

Reaper (Guardian Shadow World Book 7)

Phoenix (Guardian Shadow World Book 8)

Valkyrie (Guardian Shadow World Book 9)

**Hollister (A Guardian Crossover Series)**

Andrew (Hollister-Book 1)

Zeke (Hollister-Book 2)

**Hope City**

Hope City - Brock

HOPE CITY - Brody- Book 3

Hope City - Ryker - Book 5

Hope City - Killian - Book 8

Hope City - Blayze - Book 10

**The Long Road Home**

**Season One:**

My Heart's Home

**Season Two:**

Searching for Home (A Hollister-Guardian Crossover Novel)

STAND ALONE NOVELS

SEAL Forever - Silver SEALs

A Heart's Desire - Stand Alone

Hot SEAL, Single Malt (SEALs in Paradise)

Hot SEAL, Savannah Nights (SEALs in Paradise)

Hot SEAL, Silent Knight (SEALs in Paradise)

## ABOUT THE AUTHOR

Wall Street Journal and USA Today Bestselling Author, Kris Michaels is the alter ego of a happily married wife and mother. She writes romance, usually with characters from military and law enforcement backgrounds.

Printed in Great Britain
by Amazon